French Leave

French Leave

Sheri Cobb South

Thorndike Press • Chivers Press
Waterville, Maine USA Bath, England

This Large Print edition is published by Thorndike Press, USA and by Chivers Press, England.

Published in 2003 in the U.S. by arrangement with Prinny World Press.

Published in 2003 in the U.K. by arrangement with the author.

U.S. Hardcover 0-7862-5057-7 (Candlelight Series)
U.K. Hardcover 0-7540-8924-X (Chivers Large Print)

The text of this Large Print edition is unabridged.
Other aspects of the book may vary from the original edition.

Set in 16 pt. Plantin by Minnie B. Raven.

Printed in the United States on permanent paper.

British Library Cataloguing-in-Publication Data available

Library of Congress Cataloging-in-Publication Data

South, Sheri Cobb.
    French leave / Sheri Cobb South.
        p. cm.
    ISBN 0-7862-5057-7 (lg. print : hc : alk. paper)
    1. Nobility — Fiction.   2. England — Fiction.
3. Large type books.   I. Title.
PS3569.O755 F74 2003
    813'.54—dc21   2002038425

French Leave

1

Stranger in a strange country.
SOPHOCLES, *Oedipus at Colonus*

Paris, 1820

A haze of cigar smoke blanketed the gaming room of the Salon des Étrangers, muting the opulence of its furnishings and blurring the figures who risked fortunes at hazard or *rouge-et-noir*. In the four years he had resided on the Continent, Nigel Haversham, sixth earl of Waverly and an expatriate Englishman, was often to be found at the tables. On this occasion, however, he was content to relax in the reading room with a slightly outdated issue of the *Times*. The Salon's host, the ever-congenial Marquis de Livry, took note of this unusual state of affairs, and paused beside the earl's chair to remark upon it.

"You do not play tonight, *mon ami?*"

Lord Waverly, broaching his second

bottle of brandy, lifted one shoulder in a gesture replete with bored indifference. "Not yet. Later, perhaps."

The marquis grinned knowingly. "Ah, you are waiting for the — what do you call him? The dove?"

"Pigeon," Lord Waverly corrected him. "You will let me know when one flies in, will you not?"

"*Mais non,* milord," objected the marquis, wagging a playful finger as he moved away. "*Moi,* I am in business for myself. You will have to find your own pigeon to pluck."

Lord Waverly watched as the marquis moved from one group of guests to another, the quintessential host. The French were a hospitable race, mused Waverly, now that they had rid themselves of their penchant for beheading one another. Indeed, France made him welcome in a way his homeland no longer did, and this notorious gaming hell had become his second home. Having run deeply into dun territory, he was obliged to live by his wits — and his wits were always sharpest at the tables of the Salon des Étrangers. In point of fact, his skill at sundry games of chance had been his sole means of support since his creditors had rendered life in England too uncomfortable to be borne. And if there were other circumstances which had made life there even more intolerable, he had not allowed himself to think of those circumstances in four years, and he bloody well wasn't going to dwell on them now. He refilled his glass and turned the page of the *Times*.

He had spent some fifteen minutes thus occupied when a familiar name all but leaped off the page. Slamming his glass down on the small table at his elbow (and liberally dousing his newspaper in the process), he read the effusive account of one Ethan Brundy, Manchester mill owner, who at great risk to life and limb had almost single-handedly quelled a mob of rioting workers, and had subsequently been knighted by King George IV for his pains.

As Lord Waverly scanned the crowded lines of print, his lip curled in a derisive smile. "And so the weaver wins again," he murmured, reaching for the brandy bottle. "*Mon adversaire*, I salute you!"

A newcomer entered the salon some time later, a young man with bright eyes, rosy cheeks, and bulging pockets. Here, at last, was Lord Waverly's pigeon. But the earl, in thrall to long-suppressed memories, never saw him. The youth took his place at the hazard table without fear of being fleeced, while Lord Waverly poured the last of the brandy into his glass with a shaking hand.

He had loved her, after his fashion. He had not faulted her for marrying a wealthy Cit; such was, after all, the way of the world. He had known her father forced her into the unequal match, and had obligingly offered to relieve the monotony of her existence with a discreet *affaire du coeur*. But to be rebuffed, and for such a man? It was more than pride could bear. And now, when he had finally banished the pair of them from his thoughts, he discovered that the weaver had won through his own efforts the one thing all his wealth could not purchase: respectability. With a snort of derision, Waverly tossed off the last of the brandy in a single gulp, and called for a new bottle.

The Marquis de Livry appeared at his elbow. "I think not, milord," his host stated firmly. "You had best seek your bed. Perhaps tomorrow, *peut-être?*"

"Aye, tomorrow," Waverly conceded, his words somewhat slurred. "One day is, after all, very much like another."

Blinking owlishly, he scanned the room through bloodshot eyes. The gamesters were gone and the marquis's servants were bustling about cleaning up the mess they had left behind, the more fortunate ones delighted to find a stray counter or two underneath the green baize tables.

"I'm going to have the devil of a head in the morning," remarked the earl to no one in particular.

"Very likely," agreed the marquis, assisting his noble client to his feet.

Outside, the marquis hailed a passing hackney — one of the few still about at this advanced hour — and instructed the driver to convey Milord Waverly to his rooms in the Rue des Saint-Pères. As he watched the vehicle rattle away down the narrow street, de Livry had no doubt the earl would be back the next night, and the next. He sometimes wondered what drove the man. To be sure, Lord Waverly was not the only Englishman to patronize his establishment; since the war ended, they had come in droves, eager to lose the family fortune, and the Marquis de Livry, congenial host that he was, was happy to oblige them. He had no moral scruples about relieving his clients of inheritances which they were too stupid to salvage. But Lord Waverly was different. Jaded and debauched he might be, but he was no fool. To be sure, a woman was behind it: in the words of Fouché, *"cherchez la femme."* And the marquis, being a Frenchman, could have advised the earl that the only cure was another woman.

The hackney rolled past the art galleries and *librairies* of Saint-Germain, finally coming to a halt before an unassuming bookstore in the Rue des Saint-Pères. Waverly disembarked unsteadily and stared up at the darkened windows of his hired rooms above the shop, unwilling to return to his empty lodging and the memories which would be his only companions. Instead, he turned and walked in the other direction, neither knowing nor caring where his tottering steps might take him.

He went on in this manner for some time, until he realized he was in completely unfamiliar surroundings. The light was insufficient to determine much about his location, although he could discern a high stone wall running along the right side of the road. He was debating whether or not to turn back when suddenly his attention was caught by a furtive movement, and he beheld a pale white shadow hovering several feet above the ground. He closed his eyes, thinking perhaps he should have eschewed that second bottle of brandy, but when he opened them the mysterious entity remained, its wispy form billowing slightly in the pre-dawn breeze.

"*Arrêtez-vous!*" cried Lord Waverly, brandishing his ebony cane like a cudgel. "Who goes there?"

The apparition gave an unghostly yelp, and plummeted to the ground in a flurry of white. As if on cue, the moon broke through the clouds to reveal a small figure in the white habit and winged headdress of a young novice, collapsed in an ungainly heap.

"Now see what you have made me do!" she scolded in French as she struggled to her feet. "If *Mamère* wakes, all is lost!"

Waverly staggered forward and offered a hand to assist her in this task. As she brushed the dirt from her habit, he observed behind her a makeshift rope of torn and knotted bed sheets which dangled over the wall. Even in his inebriated state, he drew the obvious conclusion. Taking hold of the rope, he gave a pull. The knot at the end gave so suddenly that he lurched unsteadily as the length of linen tumbled into his arms.

"You had best take this," he said, bundling it up and presenting it to the novice. "I think you will not want to leave such in-

incriminating evidence behind." He felt disproportionately pleased that his tongue had barely stumbled over the word.

"*Merci, infiniment.*" Her face was as pale as her wimple in the uneven moonlight, her only distinguishable features a pair of very large and, Waverly suspected, very dark eyes. "You are most kind."

"I am not kind at all," Waverly informed her. "As a matter of fact, I am quite drunk."

"Oh," said the little nun, somewhat nonplussed by this declaration. "I will trouble you no more, *monsieur.* Again, *merci.*"

She would have flown, had Lord Waverly not caught at her sleeve.

"Wait! May I not have the honor of knowing whom I have assisted?"

She shook her head, setting the wing-like headdress flapping. "I cannot tarry! I must away before the sisters rise for matins. If I am caught — ah, *c'est insupportable!*"

"But surely your family —"

"Family? Bah! Unless I agree to marry my cousin Raoul, they will return me to the convent *comme ça!*" A snap of her fingers punctuated this pronouncement.

"Where will you go, then?" asked Waverly, curiosity penetrating his brandy-soaked brain.

The girl fixed her eyes straight ahead, and her chin assumed a mulish aspect. "I am going to Calais, and from there to England, where lives *mon grandpère*."

"A mere child, travelling alone from Paris to Calais?" the earl scoffed. "By Gad, you must be as drunk as I am!"

"I am not drunk, nor am I a child! I have almost eighteen years!"

"A veritable crone, in fact," interjected Waverly.

"Although —" Her ire faded, and she studied the earl speculatively. He found her scrutiny singularly unnerving. "— I would be most appreciative of an escort."

"I'll wager you would. Who do you have in mind?"

"You, *monsieur*."

Startled into a state approaching sobriety, Waverly wheeled about to face her. "Have you run mad? Do I look to you like a suitable companion for a child of seventeen?"

"But you are English," she insisted. "Who better to escort me to *grandpère* than one of his compatriots?"

"A sober compatriot, for one, and one who won't be beseiged by his creditors the moment he sets foot on his native soil."

"C'est un problème très difficile," admitted

the little nun. "But as I will be travelling *incognito,* it would be a very small matter to disguise your identity as well. And as for your debts, I am sure *mon grandpère* will reward you most handsomely for my safe arrival. He is very rich."

Lord Waverly hardly heard this last statement. He was thinking of the homeland he had not seen in four years, and was surprised at the intensity of the longing that assailed him.

"How much?" he asked.

"How much do you need?" she countered.

"My debts approach thirty thousand pounds," he said, not without satisfaction.

She dismissed this revelation with a wave of one small hand. "Thirty thousand pounds is as nothing to *mon grandpère.*"

"I am quite sure I will regret it in the morning, *mademoiselle,* but you just hired yourself an escort," declared the earl, bowing deeply if somewhat unsteadily. "Nigel Haversham, earl of Waverly, yours to command. And you are — ?"

She hesitated ever so slightly before saying, "I am called Marie-Thérèse."

Waverly was not deceived. "You and every other nun in France," he retorted with a skeptical snort. "If I am to help you find this grandfather of yours, you had best tell me your name."

"Very well. I am Lisette Colling."

Within the convent walls, a bell tolled. Waverly looked up at the sky and saw that it was beginning to lighten in the east.

"If you intend to remain Lisette Colling, we'd best get you away from here," he remarked, rapidly divesting himself of his greatcoat. "It is a pity you had no other clothes to wear. You could hardly be more conspicuous."

Lisette allowed Waverly to drape his greatcoat over her head, where it covered not only her habit, but the telltale headdress as well. He took her arm — although it could not be said with certainty exactly who was leading whom — and together they hurried up the street in the direction from which he had come. Lisette was quite small, Waverly noticed. Had it not been for the headdress, he supposed that her head would hardly have reached his shoulder. Helen, he recalled, was rather tall and slender as a reed.

Helen . . . Was it in the hope of seeing her again that he had agreed to this fool's errand?

He wished he knew.

He wished he had a drink.

They reached the Rue des Saint-Péres without incident and traveled along it for some distance, carefully skirting the widely spaced yellow pools of gaslight. At length Lord Waverly paused upon reaching a squat, hunched-over building whose ground floor housed a bookstore and a frame shop. The upper floors had been subdivided as living quarters, and it was to one of these which the earl led Lisette.

"Welcome to my humble abode," he said, gesturing to a dark, narrow staircase leading to the upper stories.

"Had we not best be quiet?" whispered Lisette, tiptoeing up the stairs in the earl's wake. "If someone should hear —"

"My dear child, this is not the first time I have come home at dawn with a female in tow, and I daresay it will not be the last," Lord Waverly informed her. "Our arrival would attract a great deal more attention were I to behave as if I had something —or someone — to hide."

"Oh," said Lisette, somewhat daunted by this revelation.

At the top of the stairs, Waverly withdrew a key from his pocket, unlocked a paneled door, and opened it with a flourish. Once the pair was safely inside, the earl made sure the curtains were tightly drawn, then lit a lamp. As it flared to life, Lisette examined her new surroundings. Lord Waverly's lodgings seemed to consist of two small rooms. The chamber in which they now stood appeared to serve as sitting room and dining room combined, and a doorway led from this to a smaller chamber in which Lisette could see a mahogany wardrobe and an unmade bed. Disconcerted by this innocuous piece of furniture, Lisette darted a furtive glance at her rescuer. He was quite tall and his movements, though admittedly unsteady, bespoke the languid grace of the aristocrat. His hair gleamed black in the feeble light and his eyes, regarding her with sardonic amusement, were a startling blue.

Lisette looked away in confusion. From the moment he had agreed to aid in her escape, Lord Waverly had seemed a figure from a fairy tale, and it was unthinkable that such a being should be anything but handsome. Older and wiser heads might have pointed out that any knight-errant worthy of the name should at least be sober, but Lisette had little experience with men, and so had been happily untroubled by the earl's shortcomings.

Now, however, she was obliged to admit that not everyone would view Lord

Waverly's actions in so heroic a light. If she were caught, the Mother Superior of Sainte-Marie would know exactly how to deal with a nun so steeped in depravity. She would be locked in a cell for the rest of her life and obliged to perform the ghastliest penance *Mamère* could contrive. Even if she were to escape capture, there could be no returning to her uncle's house, for Oncle Didier and Tante Simone would surely harden their hearts against a niece so lost to propriety as to run away with a strange man. She only hoped that her English grandfather would not fault her for seizing upon the only means of escape available to her.

"I don't know about you," said Lord Waverly, interrupting these melancholy reflections, "but I'm for bed."

This declaration was so exactly in keeping with Lisette's belated misgivings that her dark eyes flew open wide, and she stared at her erstwhile benefactor with an expression akin to horror.

"Acquit me of having improper designs upon your person," beseeched Waverly, torn between exasperation and amusement. "God knows I am no saint, but I am not so desperate for a woman in my bed that I am reduced to ravishing nuns!"

"*Non,* milord, of course not," Lisette said meekly.

"It is after five o'clock, and I am dead on my feet," Waverly continued. "I daresay it behooves me to offer you the bed while I take the sofa."

"*Non, pas du tout,*" Lisette hastened to assure him. "I am sure I could not shut my eyes."

The earl shrugged. "As you wish."

He disappeared into the adjoining chamber, and a moment later the thump-thump of his boots hitting the floor informed Lisette that he had lost no time in seeking his bed. She glanced toward the windows that looked down onto the Rue des Saint-Péres, wishing she had the courage to peer behind the curtains. Though she dared not for fear of being seen, a pale gray light visible through the folds suggested that sunrise was imminent. At the convent of Sainte-Marie, the sisters would be assembling for matins, and one of them would be dispatched to rouse lazy Sister Marie-Thérèse from her bed. But Sister Marie-Thérèse would not be there. Her absence would be discovered, and a hue and cry raised which would spread like wildfire throughout Paris.

Lisette stepped away from the window

and glanced toward the room where re-
posed her sleeping rescuer. He slumbered
on, apparently oblivious to the world, but
Lisette remained awake for a long time,
acutely aware of having thoroughly burned
her bridges behind her.

2

The meeting points the sacred hair dissever
From the fair head, forever and forever!
ALEXANDER POPE, *The Rape of the Lock*

Lord Waverly awoke late that afternoon with a throbbing head. Rolling over in bed, he discovered that he was fully clothed save for his boots. But greater surprises were yet in store, for the door to the sitting room was ajar, and through the open doorway could be seen a very young girl in the white habit of a novice. She was stirring sugar into a cup of steaming coffee, but upon glimpsing a movement in Waverly's room, she looked up from this task.

"Good morning, milord," she said cheerfully. "You would like some *café, oui?*"

"Who the devil are you?" demanded the earl.

The little nun laid aside her cup and regarded him in some surprise. "But do not you remember me? I am called Lisette.

23

You promised to take me to England."

Lord Waverly raked his fingers through his hair, further disarranging his raven locks. "Couldn't you see I was drunk?"

"*Oui*, so you said at the time," Lisette said placidly, retrieving her cup and sipping the warm liquid.

Waverly leaped to his feet, and instantly regretted it. The room spun crazily around him, forcing him to sit down on the edge of the bed. "And you came with me anyway? Good God, girl, have you run mad?"

"*Mais non*, milord, you were in every way the gentleman. You even offered me the bed."

"Well, that was certainly generous of me," muttered the earl. "Thank God you had the sense to refuse that offer, at any rate."

"Oh, but you assured me you were not so desperate for, ah, *la société de la femme* that you would stoop to ravishing *les religieuses*."

Waverly groaned and covered his bloodshot eyes with his hand. "I must have been even drunker than I imagined!"

"Now you would like some *café, oui*? Will you take sugar?"

"No, make it straight black," said Lord

Waverly, accepting a cup from her hand. Having drunk two cups of this reviving brew, he washed, shaved, and dressed, after which he felt more capable of facing the situation in which he now found himself.

"So I promised to take you to England," he remarked to his companion. "Did I, by any chance, happen to mention what I intended to do with you when we arrived there?"

"*Mais oui,* milord. You agreed to take me to *mon grandpère,* who will give you a reward of the most generous for your trouble."

"So this shatter-brained scheme was your idea? You relieve my mind! Now it remains only to decide how we are to smuggle you out of Paris." Lord Waverly studied Lisette for a long moment. No womanly curves were discernable beneath her shapeless habit, leading the earl to deduce that her figure was as yet undeveloped. "I think our best bet is to disguise you as a boy, and let it be known that you are my ward," he declared at the end of this inspection.

Lisette was not best pleased with this plan. "A boy, milord? *Pourquoi?* Why should your ward not be a girl?"

"Because no one in his right mind would name me ward to a girl of seventeen!"

"*Très bien*, then I will be your sister," pronounced Lisette.

"My dear child, I am thirty-five years old! You might well be my daughter!"

Lisette could not agree. "*C'est absurde!* If I were your daughter, I must have been sired when you were but seventeen!"

"Just so," the earl said darkly.

He left Lisette alone to ponder the significance of this cryptic utterance while he undertook to procure a suit of clothes befitting a boy of, he thought, about thirteen. It was while he went about this task that he first heard the rumors of a wicked girl who had escaped from the convent of Sainte-Marie on the very morning she was to have taken her vows.

Being nominally Anglican, Lord Waverly had not given much thought to what might happen to Lisette if she were captured, and he was disturbed by the whispered horrors of hair shirt and scourge. His rôle in Lisette's flight underwent a metamorphosis from the capricious lark of an inebriate to a mission which must succeed.

Having purchased a shirt, coat, trousers, shoes, and stockings, Lord Waverly stopped at the frame shop below his lodgings and requested of its proprietor the loan of a pair of shears. Lisette, fully cognizant of the need for disguise, received her new wardrobe with resignation, but questioned the necessity of the scissors.

"What do you intend to cut, milord? Are the shirtsleeves too long, perhaps?"

"Take off your headdress, Lisette," said Lord Waverly, not quite meeting her trusting gaze.

Lisette obeyed and the headdress was removed, revealing a cloud of dusky curls.

"Unpin your hair."

As realization dawned, Lisette's dark eyes grew wide with horror. "*Non,* milord, do not cut my hair! I will cover it with a hat, and no one will ever suspect!"

"They are already searching for you," Waverly informed her. "Your escape is already the talk of Paris, and God help me, I didn't know until I heard it in the streets what a price you will pay if you are caught. We cannot take foolish chances."

"But, milord —"

"No buts, my child. If you expect to reach England safely, you must do as I say."

Reluctantly, Lisette removed the pins from her hair, and the dark locks tumbled over her shoulders and down her back.

Without a word, Waverly set to with the scissors, and for a long time there was no sound in the tiny room save the metallic snip of the blades and the hushed whisper of Lisette's long hair sliding down the back of her habit to land at Waverly's feet.

"Finished," the earl pronounced at last. "It is a comfort to know that, should my skill at cards ever desert me, I can support myself as a valet."

Receiving no reply to this admittedly lame attempt at humor, he laid aside the scissors, took Lisette's chin in his hand, and tipped it up, the better to survey his handiwork. Freed of its weight, Lisette's remaining hair curled riotously about her head in a manner many a dandy required the use of curling tongs to achieve. But the earl's admiration of his *chef d'oeuvre* was cut short by the sight of Lisette's brimming eyes and tear-stained cheeks. Lord Waverly, who would have hardened his heart against hysterics, stroked her damp cheek with one finger.

"It will grow again, *ma petite*," he said gently.

"*Oui*, milord," agreed Lisette, her voice little more than a whisper.

They remained in Paris for three days,

waiting for the hue and cry surrounding Lisette's disappearance to die down. Lisette, in her boy's clothes, chafed under this forced inactivity, but Lord Waverly, while not unsympathetic, remained adamant. By day, he did his best to enliven his ward's confinement by recounting highly expurgated tales of his life in London; by night, he presented himself without fail at the Salon des Étrangers, where his skill at hazard soon won him the wherewithal to hire a post-chaise to convey them to Calais, where they might board a packet for Dover.

In exchange for one of his livelier (and more heavily edited) stories, Lord Waverly required an accounting of how she came to escape from the convent of Sainte-Marie.

"I never wished to enter the convent at all," Lisette replied candidly, "but Maman and Papa died when I was still quite young —" Waverly's lips twitched slightly at the implication that Lisette's youth lay in the distant past. "— and Oncle Didier and Tante Simone, who had taken me in, they wish me to marry *mon cousin* Raoul, who has a face like a weasel. *Quel horreur!*"

"Unthinkable!" agreed Lord Waverly, and although he shuddered visibly, his blue eyes gleamed with amusement.

"You tease me, milord, but it is quite true," Lisette chided him. "*Alors,* when I tell Raoul I will not marry him, Oncle Didier and Tante Simone say I must take the veil, for they have not the means to support me any longer. For Papa was cut off by his papa for marrying Maman, and so I have no expectations."

Waverly raised a hand to interrupt this rambling monologue. "A moment, please. I thought you said your paternal grand-father would reward me handsomely for bringing you safely to England."

Lisette's black-eyed gaze fell to her lap, and she looked the picture of guilt. "As to that, I have never met *mon grandpère,* although I know he is very rich. And," she added hopefully, looking eagerly up at the earl, "I should think that by this time he must regret most bitterly that he cast off his only son, *oui?* And be pleased to discover he has *une petite-fille?*"

Lord Waverly tried to look stern, and failed. "I see it all now! You did not escape from the convent at all. The Mother Superior undoubtedly tossed you willy-nilly over the wall!"

Lisette looked up hopefully. "Then milord is not angry?"

"On the contrary, I consider it a judgment upon me for over-imbibing."

Lisette snatched up his hand and pressed it to her lips. "Oh, I am so glad, for I have suffered agonies of guilt!"

"You will pardon me for observing that you kept your sufferings remarkably well-hidden," remarked Lord Waverly, gently withdrawing his hand from Lisette's grasp. "You are a designing minx, and I can only wonder that you went so meekly to Saint-Marie."

"Oh, but Tante Simone assured me that I did not have to stay if I did not like it. *Moi,* I know I will not like it, but Tante is sad because I will not marry her son, so I do as she wishes and go to Sainte-Marie. And I am *très misérable,* just as I expected."

"And your uncle and aunt?"

"I write to them many letters, telling them I am unhappy, but they never come for me. So the night before I am to make my vows, I stay awake all night. I tell Mamère I wish to spend the night in prayer, and she allows me to keep a candle burning in my chamber. And I do pray, but my prayers are for deliverance. Also I tear my bed sheets into strips and make for myself a rope. Then, much later, I climb up to the roof, tie my rope to the gutter, and lower myself down over the wall. That is

31

when you came along." She paused here and regarded Lord Waverly seriously. "Do you think I am very wicked, running away from the convent when it was what my uncle and aunt particularly wished?"

"My dear child," the earl was moved to declare, "I think you are quite possibly the bravest person I have ever known."

But her bravery was to be tried still further. They departed for Calais at ten o'clock in the morning, in full view of half the citizens of Paris. Lisette was all for slipping out under cover of darkness, but Lord Waverly was adamant: they would not indulge in any behavior which might be interpreted as clandestine. Lisette could not but think his dedication to this program extreme, as when he insisted not only upon stopping downstairs to pay for his lodgings and arrange to have transported to England those of his belongings which he must of necessity leave behind, but going so far as to make his young ward known to his landlady. Lisette was quite undone by this unexpected introduction, but Madame Valliers saw nothing in young Luc's manner beyond the quite natural shyness of a boy on the verge of adolescence, and so Lord Waverly and his ward boarded their hired post-chaise unmolested and were soon on their way.

"*C'est merveilleux!*" cried Lisette, removing the flat-crowned cap that covered her cropped hair. "Madame was not in the least suspicious!"

"And why should she be suspicious of a mere lad?" responded Lord Waverly, watching through the window as the post-chaise swung northward.

"I look so much like a boy?" asked Lisette, her smooth white brow furrowed in a frown. "*Vraiment,* I do not think that is a compliment!"

Lord Waverly abandoned his inspection of the passing scenery and turned to face her. "Do you want compliments, or do you want to reach your grandfather in England?"

"I want to reach *mon grandpère,*" Lisette replied without hesitation. "But if I *were* a boy, I would wish to grow up to be just such a man as you."

"Good God, why? I wouldn't wish such a fate on my worst enemy!" exclaimed Lord Waverly, rendered extremely uncomfortable by the soft glow lighting Lisette's dark eyes. "I am no hero to be adulated, Lisette. You would do well to bear it in mind."

Lisette would have argued the point, but

seeing the forbidding expression on her guardian's face, she wisely held her tongue. For the next eight hours, the post-chaise bowled steadily northward, stopping at intervals to exchange the winded and sweating horses for fresh cattle. Each of these delays was a fresh agony for Lisette, impatient as she was to put the choppy waters of the Channel between herself and the convent of Sainte-Marie. She bore it all, however, with stoic fortitude until they reached the city of Amiens, where Lord Waverly announced his intention of procuring a meal and a room for the night.

"Mais non!" cried Lisette, her expressive eyes growing round with alarm. "Better that we should press on to Arras."

"Arras? Nonsense, child! It would take another five hours or more."

"Five hours is not so very much —" Lisette began, only to be cut short.

"Now, look here," said Lord Waverly sternly, "you're the one who invited me along on this little jaunt, and if you want me to get you to England safely, you'll be quiet and let me do it my way!"

"Oui, milord," Lisette said meekly.

Accordingly, she made no demur when they drew up before a bustling posting-house, but donned her boys' cap and followed Lord Waverly from the chaise. The inn yard fairly bustled with activity, most of which appeared to be centered around a small bowling-green where gathered more than a score of men of all ages and social situations. As a quartet of men took turns rolling small wooden *boules* across the green, the various members of the group either cheered or groaned, according to the fate of their favorites.

"We seem to have arrived on tournament-day," remarked Waverly, who had not lived in France for four years without becoming acquainted with the national sport.

Lisette vouchsafed no response beyond an anxious glance at the *boules* players, but entered the posting-house in Lord Waverly's wake. The inside, too, was crowded, and Waverly was not surprised when his request for two adjacent rooms was denied.

"*Mille pardons,* milord, I don't have an empty room to boast of," said the *hôtelier* with some satisfaction, for he could tell at a glance that his patron was one of those debt-ridden Englishmen who had crossed the Channel in droves since *le petit général* had been banished to an ignominious exile on St. Helena.

Waverly accepted this disappointment

with equanimity, drawing a golden *louis* from his pocket. "A pity," he said, turning the coin over in his hand. "I must hope for better luck at the *Lion d'Or*. Come, Luc."

Whether it was the sight of the gold coin, in such short supply since the Revolution, or the mention of a rival establishment that jogged his memory, mine host suddenly bethought himself of a spare chamber which he had, until that moment, quite unaccountably forgotten. This he offered to Lord Waverly, along with his sincere regrets that he had no second chamber to offer milord's companion. Would milord and the young gentleman perhaps desire a private parlour in which to dine?

Recalling the boisterous group outside, Lord Waverly was sorely tempted. But he was determined not to act in any way secretive, and so he opted for the coffee-room, secure in the conviction that by the time the athletes finished toasting the health of the winners and drowning the sorrows of the losers, not one of them would notice a woman if she danced naked upon the table.

He allowed the innkeeper to usher them to a table in the coffee-room and to place before them a bottle of the local wine and a pair of glasses. Lisette downed her wine greedily and reached for the bottle.

"Are you sure that is wise, *enfant?*" asked Lord Waverly, observing this action with a raised eyebrow.

"You forget that I am French, milord," she said, lifting her chin. "*Sans doute,* I could drink you under the table, if I wished."

"Be that as it may, I do not think this is the time to put it to the test," Waverly replied, firmly moving the bottle out of her reach.

"You only say that because —" Lisette broke off abruptly, her frightened gaze fixed on some point over Waverly's left shoulder.

"What is it?" he asked, resisting the urge to turn around. "What is the matter?"

"It — it appears the tournament is over, milord."

Indeed, the door to the tap-room had opened to admit some half-dozen young bucks, all arguing animatedly about the game just ended.

"You are a great fool, Henri," one informed another in tones of disgust. "Why did you not fire at the cork, *hein?*"

"You must have known your point would be off the mark," concurred another.

"*Mais non!*" cried the wronged Henri,

launching into an impassioned defense of his skill.

Lord Waverly nodded at the group as they came abreast of his table, wondering what about them Lisette had found so frightening. The players returned his nod, most affording his youthful companion only the most cursory of glances before passing on. One, however, lingered long enough to favor Lisette with a piercing stare, then hurried to catch up with his cronies.

Waverly, observing this exchange and noting his companion's pale countenance, said briskly, "The hour is far advanced, Luc, and you should be in your bed."

"*Oui,* milord," Lisette murmured, casting him a grateful look as she rose from the table.

After she had gone, it was but a moment before the *boules* player returned to Lord Waverly's table.

"A handsome lad," remarked the Frenchman, eyeing the earl speculatively. Several years Waverly's junior, he possessed a pair of close-set, narrow eyes, a longish nose, and a pointed chin. "A relative, perhaps?"

Lord Waverly had supposed Lisette's unflattering description of her cousin to be figurative, but now realized that she had spoken quite literally. "My ward. And handsome, yes, but a bit more prettified than I would like. It is to be hoped that a few years at sea as a midshipman will make a man of him. Will you sit and have a drop?" he asked, indicating the bottle of wine.

The Frenchman demurred, pleading the necessity of returning to his friends, and took his leave. Lord Waverly let out a long breath and forced himself to remain at the table over another glass of wine before joining Lisette upstairs.

"Well, you insufferable brat," he said, shutting the door of their shared chamber, "there is a young man below who takes an uncommon interest in you. Have you any idea why?"

Lisette nodded. "It is *mon cousin*, Raoul. Did I not say he had a face like a weasel?"

"Your cousin is here? I thought your family was fixed in Paris!"

"*Mais non!* I never said my family was in Paris. They live in Amiens, where Oncle Didier is *un avocat*. You must have assumed they lived in Paris because that is where my convent was," she added helpfully.

"Do you realize how close we came to

being discovered back there?" demanded Lord Waverly, livid with anger and badly frayed nerves.

"*Oui*, I feared as much," confessed Lisette. "That is why I wished to go on to Arras."

"Well, why the devil didn't you say so?"

"I tried, but you told me to be quiet and let you do it your way," she reminded him.

"Do you have to obey every word I say?"

"*Mais oui*, because I am so grateful to you for taking me to *mon grandpère*."

"The more fool you," growled Lord Waverly, and headed for bed without another word.

3

An injury is much sooner forgot
than an insult.
PHILLIP DORMER STANHOPE,
EARL OF CHESTERFIELD,
Letters to His Son

They left Amiens the next morning while the
boules players were still sleeping off the previous evening's celebrations, and so departed unmolested for Arras. Here fortune
smiled upon them, for Lord Waverly found
an *hôtel* off the Grande Place which could
offer the travelers separate rooms. Not,
Waverly reflected ruefully, that such a con-
sideration mattered any longer; Lisette had
already been so long in his company that,
were she to be recognized as a female at this
point, her reputation would be ruined beyond redemption. But here, too, their luck
held, for no one took notice of them at all
beyond the idle curiosity afforded any foreign traveler.

By the time they had reached Calais, Waverly had begun to breathe easier, and Lisette had lost the hunted expression she had worn since their first encounter outside the Convent Sainte-Marie. As they boarded the packet to Dover, she fairly danced up the ladder in her eagerness to cast off. The earl, finding her enthusiasm perfectly suited to a boy of thirteen, made no attempt to dampen her high spirits, but watched in tolerant amusement as she darted below deck to inspect their quarters.

As he awaited her return, Lord Waverly fixed his eyes on the watery horizon and contemplated his return to his native soil. His reverie was at length interrupted by the sound of his own name, spoken in a distinctly British accent.

"Why, Lord Waverly, as I live and breathe!" cried his countryman, clapping him heartily on the back.

"Well met, Sedgewick," Waverly responded, recognizing the stout, over-dressed Englishman as a fellow member of White's. "I had no idea you were in France."

Sedgewick nodded. "Aye, these two months and more. But what of you? Never say you are returning to England!"

Lord Waverly cocked one eyebrow. "You would have me lie?"

"Why, how comes this about? I wasn't aware that Ethan Brundy had died!"

Sedgewick laughed heartily at his own joke, but Waverly bared his teeth in a feral grin. "The last man to mention that name in my presence received a ball to his shoulder in the Bois de Boulogne."

"I beg your pardon, my lord!" said his compatriot, more than a little affronted. "It would appear you have left your sense of humor in Paris!" he added before hurrying away, already planning how best to recount this shocking encounter to the members of White's.

Lord Waverly turned away from Sedgewick's retreating form, and found Lisette staring at him with wide eyes and a round "O" of a mouth.

"Milord!" she cried. "Did you challenge the English milord to the duel?"

"Not at all," Waverly assured her. "He had the good sense to take his leave rather than risk giving me further provocation."

"But — but what was it about?"

"Need you ask? A lady, of course," said the earl.

Lisette stared down at the weathered planks of the deck. "This lady, she must

43

have been very beautiful, *n'est-ce pas?*"

"Very."

"And you wished to marry her, *oui?*"

"She was already married. I merely wished to entice her away from her husband. When she rebuffed me, I tried my hand at extortion, with the happy result of driving her into his arms. I told you I was no hero to be adulated," he added with a wry grimace.

If this revelation served to dampen Lisette's spirits, such an unhappy state did not last long. She was too young and too sanguine of disposition to brood indefinitely, and would, indeed, have found it difficult in any case to remain downcast on such a day. The Channel crossing was ever rough, but to Lisette, the unsteady dip and rise of the deck below her feet only added to the spirit of adventure. The sun danced in and out among scudding clouds, casting sparkling reflections on the waves, and Lisette, leaning forward over the railing for a better look, found herself seized firmly by the collar.

"Gently, brat," advised Lord Waverly. "I have no intention of fishing you out of the Channel, so you'd best have a care."

Lisette smiled up at him, and the earl, observing her bright eyes and ruddy, wind-kissed cheeks, could only wonder that her cropped hair and boys' clothes had fooled anyone.

Four hours after boarding the packet, they disembarked in Dover, where Lord Waverly procured for them a nourishing repast.

"All right, brat," said the earl, noting with some amusement that the sea voyage had left Lisette's appetite unimpaired, "you are in England now. Where do we find this grandfather of yours?"

"Ah, but milord, I do not know."

"You *don't know?*" demanded Lord Waverly with lowering brow.

"*Mais non!* I have never been to England, so how could I know? But you! You are English, so *naturellement* I assumed —"

"My child, I am truly humbled by your faith in me, but I must point out that there are a few people in England whom I have never met!"

"Oh," said Lisette, momentarily daunted.

"You are clearly a judgment upon me," declared Lord Waverly, dashing a hand over his eyes. "As God is my witness, I will never again touch anything stronger than claret! Pray tell me, what, if anything, *do* you know of your grandfather?"

"I know his name is Robert, for Papa hoped to name me after him, but Mama thought Roberta was a name very ugly, and said *Grandpère* did not deserve that I should be named after him, on account of his having cast off Papa." Her brow puckered as a new thought occurred to her. "I know he was a soldier, like Papa, and I know he hated the French, for he has never forgiven Papa for marrying *une françoise*. I also know that he must be very rich, for he cut Papa off without a sou, and unless he had great many of them, such a thing would not matter, *n'est-ce pas?*"

The earl, following this speech with an effort, understood only that his promised reward had very likely no more substance than the proverbial castles in Spain. Nevertheless, it was all he had to go on, and so he betook himself to the nearest bookstore, where he spent several hours poring over a tome entitled *Stevenson's Guide to the Great Houses of England.*

"We are bound for Lancashire," he informed Lisette upon his return. "It appears your grandfather — who holds the rank of colonel, by the way — occupies a property there by the name of Colling Manor."

They set out northward that very afternoon in a hired post-chaise. It had been four days since they left Paris; the trip to Lancashire required another three, and by the time the carriage at last rattled to a stop before Colling Manor, they had been traveling for more than a se'ennight. The sun was setting over the lowlands of western Lancashire, and Lisette, whose excitement over the coming reunion had at last spent itself, had drifted into sleep, her head lolling upon Lord Waverly's shoulder. As the postilion leaped down to open the carriage door, Waverly gave his companion a gentle shake.

"Wake up, child, we're here."

Lisette sat upright and leaned across him to look out the window. Colling Manor was an imposing structure dating to the Jacobean era, with a pilastered façade ornamented with strapwork and punctuated at intervals with pointed arch windows. At present, these were decked in black crape, giving the house a forbidding aspect.

"It — It looks as if *Grandpère* is not at home," Lisette said uncertainly.

"Let's go see, shall we?"

He yielded to the urge to cup her elbow in his hand as she stepped down from the chaise, and side by side they mounted the steps to the portico. Here they found the door knocker also swathed in black. Waverly was suddenly conscious of a chill in spite of the warmth of his sleeve where Lisette's head had lain. He raised the knocker and let it fall, then, fearful that its muted thud might not be heard within, stripped off his gloves and rapped sharply on the door. A moment later it swung open to reveal a cadaverous-looking butler wearing a black armband over the sleeve of his dark suit.

"Yes?" he uttered in sepulchral tones.

"Lord Waverly to see Colonel Colling," the earl informed him.

"I fear that is impossible, your lordship," responded the butler. "Colonel Colling died ten days ago."

❦

"It will be dark soon," said Lisette, after they had climbed back into the chaise and left Colling Manor behind.

"Thank you for that observation," Waverly replied tartly.

"What will we do now?"

"My dear child, I haven't the faintest idea," said the earl with less than perfect truth. He had a very fair idea of where this adventure would end, and was equally certain that he would not be pleased with his fate. "Our first concern must be finding a place to stay for the night, and then in the morning we can —"

The carriage lurched drunkenly to the right, and Waverly broke off abruptly on an English word Lisette had never heard before. One look at his thunderous countenance, however, was enough to give her a very fair suspicion of its probable meaning, and she wisely forbore requesting a definition. Waverly sprang down to assist the coachman, and a moment later returned to help Lisette descend from the crippled vehicle.

"The rear axle is broken," he said. "I've sent the coachman and postilion to see to its repair, while I find a place for you to stay the night. I seem to recall seeing a gate some distance back; perhaps we can get help there."

They trudged over a mile before seeing the gate Waverly had remembered and, finding it open, followed the gravel drive to a large stucco edifice edged with iron railings in the Italian style, its tall, well-lit windows casting welcoming pools of light onto the manicured lawn. A greater contrast to the colonel's dreary abode would have been difficult to imagine. Once again Lord Waverly knocked on the door, and once again it was opened to him by a stately-looking butler.

"Is your master in?" Waverly asked this promising personage. "We've met with an accident on the road, and I wonder if he might assist us."

"And who shall I tell him is calling?"

Lord Waverly glanced at Lisette and hesitated, remembering all too well his ignominious flight from England and the peculiar circumstances in which he and his companion now found themselves. Until he discovered whose house he had stumbled upon, discretion, he decided, was the better part of valor.

"If you will take me to your master, I think I had best present myself directly to him."

The butler recognized in the visitor's voice the tone of one who will brook no argument and, except for muttering something about its being "highly irregular," made no demur, but allowed the two visitors to follow him up the stairs to the first-floor drawing room. The door to this chamber was closed, and when the servant opened it to announce the caller, Lord Waverly was rewarded with a glimpse of his would-be host.

In the middle of the room, a man in his shirtsleeves crawled about on the floor with a pair of curly-haired tots, both squealing with delight, riding astride his back. The butler's entrance caused the beast of burden to look up, and Lord Waverly, recognizing his host, was startled into exclamation.

"Good God! Not *you!*"

❦

It was not, thought Sir Ethan Brundy, the most distinguished manner in which to confront one's mortal enemy for the first time in over four years. Easing his twin passengers to the floor, he rose to his feet and reached for the coat tossed carelessly across the back of a striped satin chair.

The children, sensing that their fun was at an end, were much inclined to cling to their father's coattails, the firstborn, Master Charles Brundy, going so far as to regard the unwelcome visitor with accusing brown eyes and a lower lip thrust forward in a pout. His brother, Master William Brundy, the younger by some twelve minutes and ever the more vocal of the two, was more direct.

" 'oo's dat man?" he demanded of his parent, pointing a pudgy finger at the invader.

" 'ush, Willie," chided his father. "Lord Waverly is an old — acquaintance."

51

"What's 'e doing 'ere?" persisted Willie.

"I'd like to know that meself," said Sir Ethan. "Run along to your mama, Willie. You too, Charlie."

Master Charles obeyed, albeit reluctantly, but Willie Brundy was made of sterner stuff. "I want to stay with you," he insisted, tugging at the tail of his father's baggy coat.

Sir Ethan scooped the lad up into his arms, then turned back to regard the earl suspiciously. "I thought you were still in France, Waverly. What brings you 'ere?"

"Not the pleasure of your company, I assure you," drawled Waverly. "In fact, it took nothing less than a broken axle to, er, propel me to your door."

Sir Ethan was spared the necessity of a reply by the entrance of his wife of four years, a honey-haired beauty bearing yet another dark-haired child, this one still in leading strings.

"Emily is so fussy, darling, do you suppose she could be cutting another —" But Emily's teething woes were forgotten as she recognized the elder of the two callers. A wealth of shock and revulsion were contained in one word: *"Waverly!"*

"Lady Helen, your very obedient," he said silkily, sweeping her an elegant leg. He bent his quizzing-glass upon the three children, then added in a bored drawl, "I have thought of you often over the past four years, my dear, but not once did I imagine you as the mother of no less than three weaver's brats."

"Four, actually," said Lady Helen with some satisfaction. "The baby is napping."

Waverly turned and trained his quizzing-glass upon the proud papa. "Do try for a little restraint, Mr. Brundy," recommended the earl. "Overzealousness is the curse of the lower classes."

"I daresay you will not have heard, living abroad, but Mr. Brundy is properly addressed as Sir Ethan," said Lady Helen, chin held high.

"We won't stand on ceremony with 'is lordship, me dear." Sir Ethan set Master William on his feet and sent him to his mama with a gentle swat to the derriere. "Take the children upstairs, 'elen. I'll be along directly."

Lady Helen cast an uncertain glance at her husband and, receiving her answer in that method of silent communication peculiar to married couples, took her son by the hand. "Come along, William, you heard your father."

By tacit agreement, neither man spoke

until the door had closed behind Lady Helen and her children. Then Lord Waverly addressed his host. "Look here, I know this is deuced awkward, but I'd be most grateful if you could give my ward and me a room for the night." As if fearing a rejection, he hastened to add, "I think you know I would not ask for such a favor were it not absolutely necessary."

Though not gently born, Sir Ethan was an astute man, and he received the strong impression that there was more to Lord Waverly's story than he was telling. Seeing the earl's almost imperceptible nod in the direction of his young ward, Sir Ethan surmised the reason for Waverly's reticence.

"You look fagged out," he spoke kindly to the youth, who had been following the conversation with a baffled expression, much like one who enters the theatre during the second act of the play. "I'll 'ave the 'ousekeeper show you to one of the guest rooms."

He suited the word to the deed, and in a very short space of time a plump, matronly woman bore Lisette off with the promise of a plate of biscuits and a hot brick for her bed. Alone with his adversary, Sir Ethan regarded the earl expectantly.

"Will you 'ave a drop of brandy, Waverly?"

Waverly would have accepted, but bethought himself of his vow. "Have you any claret instead?"

Sir Ethan raised his eyebrows at this unexpected request, but decanted the preferred liquid into a glass and handed it to his guest.

"Now, I wonder what sort of mischief you're up to, that you'd turn up on me doorstep after all this time?"

"Mischief?" echoed the affronted earl. "I assure you, I spoke no less than the truth when I said I'd had a carriage accident. And why you would suppose my motives to be dishonorable —"

"I daresay I was unduly influenced by the fact that you once kidnapped me wife," Sir Ethan offered by way of apology.

"*Au contraire*," protested Waverly. "Lady Helen entered my domicile of her own free will."

"Aye, but would she 'ave left it in like manner, if I'd not intervened?"

"Probably not, but this is all water under the bridge. If you must know, I'm in the devil of a coil. You will no doubt be surprised to learn that my 'ward' is, in fact, a young lady."

Far from registering shock, Sir Ethan received this revelation without batting an eye. "Knowing you the way I do, I must say that doesn't surprise me in the least."

"I am doing my damnedest to prevent her becoming a nun!"

"You'd be the man to do it, too," agreed Sir Ethan with a nod.

"It isn't at all what you think!" growled the earl. "I discovered her escaping from a French nunnery, and I agreed to escort her to her grandfather in England."

"Foxed, were you?" remarked Sir Ethan knowingly.

"Completely castaway, but that's neither here nor there. We arrived at Colling Manor only to discover that the Colonel had died."

"Aye, almost a fortnight ago."

Lord Waverly heaved a sigh. "I shall have to marry the girl, I suppose."

"I can't see as 'ow she's done anything as bad as all that!" objected Sir Ethan.

"*Touché!*" said Waverly, acknowledging this hit by lifting his glass. "I assure you, I am fully aware of my unsuitability as husband to a child of seventeen! But what would you? If her grandfather had been alive, he and I might have concocted a story to satisfy the tabbies, but as it is, I can hardly abandon the girl."

"What's the matter, Waverly? 'ave you

developed a conscience, during all that time in France?"

"If so, I could wish otherwise, for I am finding it damned inconvenient!"

" 'as the girl no family in France?"

Lord Waverly scowled. "Her uncle practices law in Amiens, but her maternal relations are the ones who sent her to Sainte-Marie. I won't hand her back over to them."

"You'll forgive me if I 'ave an 'ard time picturing you in the rôle of knight-errant," observed Sir Ethan. "What, pray, is your interest in Colonel Colling's granddaughter?"

"If you must know, Mademoiselle Colling assured me that her grandfather would reward me handsomely for her safe arrival."

" 'is heir might do the same. 'ave you a place to stay while the colonel's solicitor could be sent for?"

"The truth is, I need more than a place to stay. I live in daily expectation of being recognized and hounded by duns." Waverly raked slender fingers through his raven locks. "Oh, the devil! In for a penny, in for a pound, I suppose. I would be much obliged to you if you would buy up my vowels."

If it had been Lord Waverly's ambition to shock his host, he achieved it with this request. "Why the deuce would I want to saddle meself with your bad debts?" demanded Sir Ethan.

"I swear you will have every farthing back at whatever rate of interest you choose. Only say you will do it! God knows you can afford it," he added bitterly.

"I'm not a cursed moneylender!" objected Sir Ethan. "If I do as you ask, it'll be as a courtesy to Miss Colling. There'll be no interest."

"Rendering me all the more beholden to you," drawled Waverly. "Lord, how you must be enjoying this!"

"Believe me, I take no pleasure in throwing good money after bad," protested Sir Ethan. Then a smile touched his lips, and he added, "But I can afford to be generous. After all, I won the lady."

4

Wedding is destiny,
And hanging likewise.
JOHN HEYWOOD, *Proverbs*

Lord Waverly did not see Lisette again until breakfast the following morning, by which time Sir Ethan had held a protracted conversation with his wife. Once she had recovered from the shock afforded her by the news of the earl's impending nuptials, Lady Helen instructed her abigail to select one of her own gowns suitable for a lady of Lisette's tender years (this from one having attained the ripe old age of five-and-twenty) and to alter it to fit her shorter figure.

And so it was that Lord Waverly, resolved to do his duty, entered the breakfast room and found himself confronting a slip of a girl in a high-waisted white muslin gown, its high neck gathered into a lace ruff which framed a piquant heart-shaped face. A matching ribbon was threaded through cropped black curls, and though her dark eyes sought his without bashfulness, a telltale flush tinted her cheeks.

"*Ah*, milord, now I am a girl again, *oui?*" she cried gaily, rising from her chair to bob a curtsy in his direction.

"It would certainly appear so," he replied, then devoted his attention to the task of filling a plate from an assortment of silver chafing dishes on the buffet.

There were only three at breakfast, Sir Ethan having eaten early and departed for town on a financial matter known only to himself and his guest. Lord Waverly, after helping himself to buttered eggs, kippers, toast, and marmalade, sat down between Lisette and Lady Helen and put forth a number of polite but meaningless queries as to the quality of their sleep and their expectations for the morning's weather. The meal passed in desultory fashion, Lady Helen being too well-bred to voice any of the questions her husband's confidences had raised, until at last she rose from the table, announcing her intention of visiting the nursery.

"Oh, may I come, too?" Lisette begged. "How I should like to see again *les enfants!*"

"And I was hoping you would explore

Lady Helen's gardens with me," Lord Waverly remarked regretfully. "Cannot your nursery visit wait until later?"

"By all means, take Waverly about the gardens," Lady Helen beseeched Lisette. "Charles is quite surly in the mornings, and William will not touch his breakfast so long as there are guests to entertain. You may play with them later, after they have eaten."

And so with his hostess's permission, Lord Waverly took Lisette's arm and led her into the carefully manicured gardens bordering the eastern side of the house.

"I do like Lady Hélène, do not you?" Lisette confided cheerfully as they made their way down a flagged walk toward a splashing fountain. "She is very beautiful, *n'est-ce pas?*"

"It would not be seemly for me to pass such a judgment on another man's wife," the earl returned noncommitally.

Lisette, however, had no such qualms. "*Moi*, I think she is beautiful. And it was very good of *Monsieur* Brundy to let us stay."

"Beautiful though she may be, Lady Helen would, I feel sure, point out to you that her husband is properly addressed as Sir Ethan."

Lisette, it seemed, had no very high opinion of her host's proper designation. "Bah! It is a name impossible to pronounce!"

Not for nothing had Lord Waverly spent four years among the French. "The English 'th' escapes you, does it?" he asked, cocking a knowing eyebrow.

"The French do not poke out our tongues when we speak," Lisette pronounced loftily.

"In the case of our host, such a gesture would be entirely appropriate," drawled the earl.

"You do not like *Monsieur* Brundy? I thought him very nice."

"To be sure, he is a paragon among men," agreed Waverly with a marked lack of enthusiasm.

"Although," added Lisette, her white brow puckered thoughtfully, "I do find his speech of a strangeness."

"Save for certain denizens of the East End whom you will not meet in the best circles, the whole of London finds his speech of a strangeness. But I did not bring you out here to discuss Lady Helen's husband."

For the first time, Lisette seemed self-conscious and ill at ease in his presence.

"*Non? Pourquoi,* then, did you bring me here?" she asked uncertainly.

Lord Waverly seated himself on a stone bench and drew Lisette down to sit beside him.

"This adventure has not ended as we planned, has it, my child?"

Lisette knew not what reply to make, but pleated a fold of her borrowed gown with fingers that shook.

"Now that your grandfather is out of the question, have you given any thought to your future?"

"I — I could give lessons in the French language," Lisette suggested.

"Impossible!"

Up came Lisette's pointed chin. "*Mais non!* I have spoken French all my life!"

"My dear girl, any prospective employer has only to look at you to see how unsuitable you are for a teaching post."

"And you, do you have a better idea?"

"I believe I do." He took her small hand and cradled it gently between his larger ones. "Lisette, would you do me the honor of becoming my wife?"

Lisette snatched her hand away and leaped to her feet. "It pleases you to mock me, milord!"

"I assure you, I was never more in earnest. I have never before offered marriage to any woman. What makes you think I would do so now in jest?"

"*Vraiment,* you cannot wish to marry me," she said uncertainly.

"I am afraid that what either of us wishes has very little to say to the matter. I warned you from the outset that I was not a suitable escort for you, but I am not such a blackguard as to leave you without protection in a strange country." He realized that, as a proposal of marriage, this declaration left much to be desired, and added more gently, "Come, Lisette, we have been through a great deal together, and understand each other very well. I can think of no reason why we should not be very happy together."

"None at all," Lisette said sadly, "except that you — that we do not love each other. But if you think it best, milord, then I will marry you."

Waverly took her hand and raised it to his lips for a chaste salute. "I will not insult your intelligence by proclaiming myself the happiest of men, but I swear I shall never give you cause to regret your decision."

Lisette was spared the necessity of a reply by the timely arrival of a liveried footman. This individual, upon discovering that he had interrupted a *tête-à-tête*, coughed, cleared his throat, coughed again, and informed the earl that Sir Ethan had returned from town and was at present in his study, where he awaited Lord Waverly's convenience.

"We shall speak more of this later," Waverly told Lisette, pressing her hand briefly before following the footman inside, leaving his affianced bride alone in the garden.

Thus left to her own devices, Lisette walked slowly over to the fountain and stood there for a long moment, gazing down at her reflection in the water.

"I am sure I must be the happiest girl in all the world," she declared aloud in her native tongue, then gave vent to her joy by bursting into tears.

🍎

Lord Waverly went straightway to the study, where he found his host absorbed in examining sample swatches of printed cotton cloth.

"Well, Brundy, what of it?" asked the earl, closing the door behind him.

Sir Ethan looked up. "You'll be 'appy to know you can move freely about Manchester without being clapped into debtor's prison," he reported.

"Happy, indeed," drawled Lord Waverly. "It has always been my ambition to cut a dash among the denizens of the industrial North. To what extent, may I ask, am I indebted to you for this achievement?"

Sir Ethan named a sum which, while high, was not nearly so exorbitant as the earl had expected.

"No more than that?" he asked. "I must admit, that is the most welcome piece of news I have received in almost a fortnight. If you've no objection to housing Mademoiselle Colling for a few days, I'll post to London and arrange for repayment."

Sir Ethan cleared his throat. "Er, I'm afraid it won't be that simple."

"Now why, I wonder, am I not surprised?" Waverly mused. "Well, go ahead, man, give me the worst."

"Your debts would've been much 'igher, but for the fact that your possessions were sold at public auction shortly after you decamped for the Continent. If you go to London, you'll 'ave to put up at Limmer's, for your 'ouse there 'as been stripped to the bare walls."

Lord Waverly raked his fingers through his hair, disarranging his ebony locks. "Damn! And my principal seat, Waverly Hall?"

"I believe your steward was able to salvage most of the heirlooms, but little else." He paused slightly, then added, "For meself, though, I'd 'ave put me blunt into making the estate profitable again, rather than throw it away on a lot of mouldy old portraits of me forebears."

"I've no doubt you would, had you any forebears to boast of," returned the earl. "Forgive my impertinence, but it strikes me of a sudden that you are remarkably well-informed regarding my affairs."

Sir Ethan's smile was wintry. "I'll not deny I've kept a weather eye out for you these last few years. I think you know why."

"Have no fear! Lady Helen has made her choice, and little though I understand it, I am prepared to abide by her decision. I loved her, you know — as much as I am capable of loving any woman."

"You'll forgive me for saying you have strange ways of showing it," was Sir Ethan's skeptical reply.

"Ah, but therein lies my fatal flaw, if you will: I am far too fond of my own comfort to sacrifice it for any female. Having judged Lady Helen necessary to my comfort, I could hardly be expected to yield to your legal claim."

"Be that as it may," remarked Sir Ethan, "it can't 'ave been comfortable for you, getting that chit out of France."

"Lest you think to credit me with a chivalry I do not possess, recall that I was drunk at the time, and that I had been promised a handsome sum for my pains." The earl grimaced. "It seems I am fittingly recompensed, for while I sincerely doubt that the promised reward will ever materialize, it appears the disturbances to my comfort have only begun. I have made Miss Colling an offer of marriage, which she has accepted. I suppose I had best lose no time in posting to London to procure a special license."

"I'll go with you," volunteered Sir Ethan.

"Pray do not trouble yourself," objected the earl, somewhat taken aback by this gesture.

" 'Tis pure self-interest," Sir Ethan assured him. "If you were to be clapped into Marshalsea, I'm not sure I could resist the temptation to leave you there."

❦

Whatever were the earl's qualms concerning his approaching nuptials, it must be said to his credit that he did an admirable job of concealing these. When, at dinner, he formally announced to the Brundys that he had made Mademoiselle Colling a proposal of marriage, and that his suit had been accepted, nothing in his demeanor would have led the casual observer to suspect that his feelings toward the union were anything but blissful.

Lady Helen, however, possessed the benefit of several years' acquaintance with Lord Waverly, during which she had arrived at a very fair estimation of his character. She received the news of his betrothal with considerable trepidation, and the sight of Mademoiselle Colling's shy blushes as she gazed up at her bridegroom did nothing to allay Lady Helen's misgivings. It was with the express intention of communicating these to Lord Waverly that she seized upon the first available opportunity to engage him in private conversation, leaving her husband to entertain the young Frenchwoman — a task for which he did not thank her, as he and Lisette had the greatest difficulty in understanding one another's accents.

"I suppose I should wish you happy upon your betrothal, Waverly, but truly, I cannot like it," Lady Helen confessed frankly, having drawn the earl aside under the pretext of displaying to him a recently completed portrait of herself, her husband, and their progeny.

Lord Waverly cocked one eyebrow. "And what, pray, do you find so objectionable about the match?"

"Need you ask?" she chided.

"I think not. But remember, my dear, you had your chance."

Spots of angry color suffused her cheeks. "I didn't mean that *I* wished to marry you!"

"Alas, I am quite cast down." Lord Waverly bent his quizzing-glass upon the painted canvas. The artist had eschewed the *faux* classical elements so much in vogue and had created instead an intimate family portrait. Lady Helen was seated on a chair with her infant daughter on her lap. Sir Ethan stood at her shoulder with the other girl in his arms, while the twin boys sat on the floor at their father's feet, playing with a small dog of indeterminate parentage. "I daresay it would be expected of me to compliment you on the beauty of your children, my dear, but honesty compels me to say that they look far too much like their father."

"If you think to change the subject by goading me to Ethan's defense, let me disabuse you of that notion," Lady Helen said roundly. "Really, Waverly, it is not well done of you. Mademoiselle Colling is much too young. She will never understand about your *chères amies.*"

Up came the earl's quizzing-glass, which he trained upon his hostess. "I find your vehemence on this subject singularly disturbing, my dear! Pray, what indiscretion has Mr. Brundy committed to engender such strong feelings on your part?"

"*Sir Ethan* has never given me any reason to question his fidelity," retorted Lady Helen, with the slightest emphasis on her husband's newly acquired title. "I wonder if your countess will say the same after four years of marriage to you?"

"I daresay I can be at least as discreet as your weaver," replied the earl, then turned back to address his host. "A flattering likeness, Mr. Brundy, but what, pray, is the significance of the mongrel dog? Is he a family pet, or is his presence meant as a symbolic statement of your ancestry?"

She recounted this conversation to her husband some time later, as they traversed the corridor to their adjoining bedchambers.

"Four years abroad have not changed Waverly in the least!" she informed Sir Ethan, her green eyes flashing angrily.

"The man is as odious as ever. Do you know, he suggested that you have been keeping a mistress?" The angry light faded, and she asked uncertainly, "You haven't have you?"

For an answer, he put his arms around her and drew her close. " 'e's trying to provoke you, love — and succeeding beautifully, I'd say."

Lady Helen sighed and rested her head against his shoulder. "I'll be glad when he's gone."

"Aye, so will I. I don't like the way he sniffs 'round you, 'elen. I never 'ave, and I never will."

She smiled provocatively up at him. "You might try sniffing 'round me yourself."

"It's tempting, love, but if I'm to prepare for a trip to London, I'd best seek me bed." Suiting the action to the word, he kissed her lightly on the lips and disappeared behind his own door.

A discontented sigh escaped Lady Helen's lips as she entered the adjacent room and closed the door. It had been this way ever since the birth of their youngest child. In every other way her husband was all devotion, but in the six months since little Catherine's arrival, he had not once come to her bed, nor invited her to his.

Lady Helen allowed her abigail to undress her, then dismissed the woman and stood examining her shift-clad form in the cheval glass. To be sure, childbirth wrought changes, but Lady Helen was fortunate in that these had been subtle, and easily remedied with moderate lacing. Even the most critical inspection revealed nothing that might have given him a disgust of her person.

The logical conclusion, then, was that he no longer loved her. But this, too, she rejected. She could still remember — though dimly, through a haze of the laudanum she had been given to ease a grueling childbirth — lying limp and exhausted on the bed while her husband knelt beside her, sobbing as if his heart were breaking. Yes, he still loved her, or at least he had done so as recently as six months ago. What, then, had happened to them?

How very like Waverly to turn up again after all these years, reminding her anew of how happy she had once been! The memories only served to make her all the more dissatisfied with the present state of her marriage. How Waverly would laugh to know how matters now stood between them! Yes, *he* was responsible for putting into her head the ridiculous notion that her husband no longer loved her, that he might even be keeping a mistress.

It was not until much later, just before sleep claimed her, that she remembered he had never denied it.

5

The woman's a whore,
and there's an end on't.
SAMUEL JOHNSON,
from James Boswell, *Life of Johnson*

Upon the morrow, Lord Waverly went in
search of his betrothed and found her upstairs in the nursery, sitting on the rug and
stacking wooden blocks with the brothers
Brundy.

"*Bonjour,* milord," she said cheerfully
upon seeing him enter. "I am watching *les
enfants* while Nurse prepares for them *le
petit déjeuner.*"

Master William seized the opportunity
afforded by the distraction to knock the
blocks down, a violation of the rules of fair
play so flagrant as to make Master Charles
howl in protest.

" 'e's crying," Willie self-righteously informed the newcomer, pointing at his wail-
ing brother.

"Willie, you naughty boy!" scolded Lisette, scrambling to collect the scattered wooden cubes. "Now you have made Charlie cry. Pick him up, milord, *s'il vous plaît.*"

Lord Waverly eyed the miniature Sir Ethan with distaste, but dutifully grasped the sobbing child by the armpits and lifted him, all the while holding him at arm's length. "Good heavens, what a repellent child! What do I do with it?"

"Mais non!" cried Lisette, laughing as she clambered to her feet to relieve the earl of his burden. "He is not a sack of meal!"

Waverly surrendered the child with no small sense of relief, and Master Charles was soon settled in Lisette's arms.

"Ah, milord, are they not the dearest things?" said Lisette, laying her cheek against Charles's soft black curls.

"Undoubtedly," agreed the earl, suppressing a shudder.

"Moi, I wish *I* had a —" she broke off, blushing, and when Nurse entered the room to announce that breakfast was ready, Lisette, in her embarrassment, all but fell on the good woman's neck. *"Ah, c'est prêt!* I have promised the children that I will eat with them. Will you join us, milord?"

"I fear I must decline. I should like to have a word with you in private, Lisette."

Recognizing her cue, Nurse set the tray on the table and bustled away, muttering something about having forgotten the butter for the twins' bread. Waverly waited until the door closed behind her, then turned to address his betrothed.

"First of all," he said, choosing his words with care, "it appears my offer of marriage was rather ambiguous. I should have made it plain that the sort of marriage I propose is one in name only — what the French call a *mariage blanc*."

"But — but what if I do not wish to have a *mariage blanc?*"

"My dear child, you must trust me to know what is best for you," said Waverly with some asperity. "You are far too young to be tied to a man twice your age — particularly a man who has led the sort of life I have lived."

"But you will want an heir, *non?*" Lisette persisted, absently running her fingers through Charles's curls.

"I have a younger brother in the army and another attached to the British embassy in Russia. Surely between the pair of them, they can contrive to save the family from extinction."

"Voyons!" cried Lisette, all sparkling eyes and flushed cheeks. "You wish to marry me, but still I will live like a nun. For this I might have stayed at Sainte-Marie!"

"Nonsense! You will have the title of Countess and all the privileges that your rank and my name can offer. You shall wear fine clothes and attend parties every night, if that is what you wish."

Lisette shrugged her slender shoulders. *"Très bien.* I shall be a very gay and well-dressed nun."

"Don't be ridiculous!" Lord Waverly, who had never been overly burdened by scruples where such matters were concerned, found it unaccountably embarrassing to discuss them with the young lady who was soon to be his wife. "We will speak more of these things when you are rather older. But consider for a moment that by the time you are twenty, I will be almost forty, and you will no doubt prefer a man nearer your own age. For now, suffice it to say that, when the time comes, you will not find me unreasonable, so long as you are discreet. And I, for my part, will conduct my own *amours* so as to spare you any embarrassment."

Lisette might have argued the point, but seeing that Lord Waverly's mind was made up, lapsed into somewhat sulky silence.

"Now that *that* is settled," the earl said briskly, "I came up to tell you I must make a brief journey to London."

"You are going away? But you will take me with you, *oui?*" asked Lisette, her dark eyes wide with alarm.

Waverly shook his head. "Not this time."

"Is it because you are angry with me, milord? If so —"

"Angry with you, Lisette?" he echoed, smiling slightly. "I do not think I could be — at least, not for long."

"Is it because you have compromised me? But I can be once again your Cousin Luc, and no one will ever know!"

The earl shook his head. "I am sorry, child, but Cousin Luc has died an unlamented death. You may join me in London within a fortnight. In the meantime, I will procure a special license, and we may be wed immediately upon your arrival."

"You would leave me here all alone?"

Waverly had to smile at this description. "Not at all. There are the children to play with, you know, and I believe Lady Helen intends to take you to her dressmaker. I daresay you will enjoy yourself hugely."

Lisette, fighting tears, could only shake her bowed head.

"Come, *ma petite*," he added, taking her chin in his hand and tilting her head back. "It will not be for long, I promise. You will join me very soon, and if you wish, I will take you to Astley's Amphitheatre to see the equestrian performer. Now, if you will excuse me, I must see to the packing of my bags."

"Equestrian performers," Lisette repeated to her young playmate after the earl had gone. "Bah! He thinks I am no older than — than you or Willie. But I will show him! I will give him an heir, *oui*, and a little girl, too. And when you are quite grown up, you shall marry her."

Master Charles Brundy, displeased with this vision of his future, began to howl anew.

❧

Lord Waverly and Sir Ethan departed for London the next day, and within a fortnight had managed to rectify the worst of the earl's embarrassments. A successful evening at a Jermyn Street gaming house had won for Waverly the wherewithal to make his town house habitable for himself and his bride, and it remained only for him to procure a special license. With this end in view, he betook himself to Doctors' Commons and the London office of the

Archbishop of Canterbury, where he paid the requisite fee of £5 to the aging cleric who assisted the archbishop in this capacity.

"Names?" requested this worthy, dipping his quill into the inkstand.

"Nigel Haversham, sixth earl of Waverly."

"Ah, Lord Waverly! I was at Oxford with your father many years ago, although he was still Viscount Melling at the time. And the lady's name?"

"Lisette Colling, spinster, of Amiens."

The clergyman looked up, revealing pale blue eyes behind small round spectacles. "French?"

Waverly nodded.

"And the lady is of legal age?"

Waverly hesitated over the question, which he had failed to anticipate. None but a fool could look at Lisette and believe her to be twenty-one years of age. There was nothing for it but to tell the truth.

"No, she is not quite eighteen."

"And you have some proof of parental consent?"

"Alas, her parents, one of whom was English, are dead," the earl confessed.

"But she must have had a guardian in France," persisted the cleric.

Mentally cursing himself for failing to anticipate the legal complications inherent in marrying a young lady half one's age, Waverly assumed a soulful expression. "As to that, it is a most romantic story," he said with a melancholy sigh. "I rescued her from a Parisian convent with the intention of bringing her to her English grandfather, only to discover that the gentleman had died a scant ten days earlier. Of course, by that time we had formed so violent a fondness for each other that we could not bear to be torn apart."

"And her French guardian?" prompted the cleric, unmoved by Waverly's burst of eloquence.

"Perhaps you did not understand: her French guardians placed her in a nunnery against her will," said Waverly, certain that this circumstance must touch the bishop's Protestant soul.

"It is a great pity," clucked the older man, shaking his head sympathetically. "Nevertheless, she cannot wed without their consent. Unless —"

"Yes?" prompted the earl.

"If she is indeed half English, you might apply to the Lord Chancellor for an English guardian to be named."

"Impossible! We cannot wait that long!"

The clergyman blinked at him, and Waverly, startled by his own vehemence, resumed his soulful tone once more. "Surely some allowance must be made for the natural impatience of a man in love."

"Unfortunately, my lord — or perhaps fortunately — our laws were not written by men in love," the cleric pointed out. "Without the consent of her guardian, there can be no marriage, at least not until Miss Colling turns twenty-one."

"You expect us to wait *four years?*"

"It is not so very long," said the clergyman soothingly. "The Good Book tells us Jacob waited fourteen years for Rachel."

Lord Waverly might have retorted that Jacob had not been obliged to play nursemaid to Rachel in the interim, but he swallowed this fruitless rejoinder and cast about in his mind for a solution. He had nothing with which to bribe the man, even if he could have been sure the cleric was open to that particular form of persuasion. And then, quite unexpectedly, inspiration struck.

"I daresay you are right," Waverly admitted with a sigh of resignation. "Little though I like it, I must thank you for your wise counsel, Mr. — ?"

"Fairchild. Robert Fairchild, happy to be

of service, my lord."

Waverly's eyes opened wide. "Ah, *Robert* Fairchild, is it? But of course! My father mentioned you on occasion. As I recall, he once observed that nothing in your early career would have indicated a promising future as a respected churchman." He gave the clergyman a knowing smile. "Indeed, there were one or two incidents which might have suggested quite the opposite, were there not?"

Mr. Fairchild turned alarmingly pale, and Lord Waverly knew that he had drawn a bow at a venture and somehow managed to find a mark.

"How my father would laugh, could he see what a paragon of virtue you have become," continued the earl, pressing his advantage. "It is almost too good a story to keep to oneself, is it not? I wonder what the Archbishop would make of it!"

On this faintly sinister note, he once again thanked Mr. Fairchild for his trouble, bade him good day, and started toward the door, still chuckling to himself. He had just laid his hand on the knob when Mr. Fairchild called out.

"Wait!"

Waverly turned back, his eyebrows arched in mild surprise. "Yes, Mr. Fairchild?"

The clergyman swallowed convulsively. "It just occurred to me — if Miss Colling has been under your protection —" He broke off, flushing, at the unfortunate implication of his words. "— That is, if you have been responsible for Miss Colling's well-being since her departure from France — what I am trying to say is, one might conceivably argue that *you* are her guardian, might they not?"

"I have certainly considered myself so."

"That being the case, my lord, it would be ludicrous to think that you would withhold your consent to her marriage to yourself —"

"Utterly ludicrous," agreed the earl.

"Yes, well, given the unusual circumstances, perhaps —"

Lord Waverly left Doctors' Commons within the quarter-hour, bearing a special license in his pocket.

While Lord Waverly practiced blackmail upon the clergy, Sir Ethan was left to his own devices. For this circumstance he could only be thankful, as he had certain affairs of his own to attend to, the delicate nature of which made it desirable that they be settled before his wife's arrival in Town.

To this end, he set out from his town residence in Grosvenor Square, and hailed a hackney. He was set down a short time later in front of a neat but unpretentious dwelling in Green Street. He had never been here before, but he had heard a great deal about the house and its principal occupant. He looked up at the first-floor windows, their curtains pulled tightly closed, and ran a finger underneath a cravat that suddenly felt too tight. Then, taking a deep breath, he mounted the stairs, raised the brass knocker mounted in the center of the paneled door, and allowed it to fall.

A moment later the door opened to reveal a shutter-faced butler in dignified black. "Yes?" intoned this well-trained individual in disinterested accents.

"I — I'd like to see Mrs. 'utchins, if you please."

"And whom may I say is calling?"

Sir Ethan reached for his card case, then decided it was probably wisest not to leave evidence of his visit. "Ethan Brundy — *Sir* Ethan Brundy," he added a bit more confidently. He was not entirely comfortable with that "Sir Ethan" nonsense, but it had not taken him long to discover that a title had its uses.

Sure enough, the butler stepped back to

allow him entrance, then led him to a morning room adjoining the hall. While he waited for his hostess's arrival, Sir Ethan studied his surroundings. The room, while not large, was tastefully decorated in airy blue and white. So far there was nothing to suggest that this house had seen even half of the goings-on with which rumor credited it.

"Well, well, so *you* are Sir Ethan Brundy," drawled a low-pitched feminine voice.

Sir Ethan turned toward the sound and blinked in surprise. He had not known quite what to expect of one of London's most expensive courtesans, but the woman standing before him might have been any one of a dozen Society matrons. She was a handsome woman, a bit closer to forty than to thirty. Skillfully applied rouge and kohl did an admirable job of preserving what remained of what must have once been a stunning beauty. Her well-endowed figure was fashionably clad in an elegant morning gown not unlike those currently hanging in his own wife's clothes-press. The discovery was somehow reassuring. Sir Ethan let out his breath, instantly more at ease.

"Mrs. 'utchins," he said, bowing over her

hand. "Forgive me for calling without 'aving been introduced —"

"Not at all," she assured him, gesturing toward one end of a camel-backed sofa as she sank gracefully down onto the other end. "Do sit down! I have heard all about you, and read of your recent heroics in the *Times*. No further introduction is needed. Now, what may I do for you?"

The question itself was innocent enough, but Sir Ethan flushed scarlet nonetheless, his newfound confidence utterly deserting him. He sat down beside her and launched into explanation. "You see, Mrs. 'utchins, I've a problem —"

"There is no need for embarrassment, Sir Ethan," she assured him. "Many of the gentlemen who come to me have problems. I do my best to help them," she added with a provocative smile.

If it were possible, Sir Ethan's countenance grew even redder. "It's not — that sort of problem. I want — information."

Mrs. Hutchins arched one sculpted eyebrow. It was not the first time a gentleman had come to her for educational purposes, but these seekers after enlightenment were generally quite a bit younger. " 'Information,' sir?" she prompted.

"Aye. 'Tis about me wife."

"I see," said Mrs. Hutchins, nodding in sympathy. "She doesn't understand you, I daresay."

"Oh, she understands me well enough. But we've 'ad four children in as many years —"

"I congratulate you," purred Mrs. Hutchins, her carmined lips curving as she looked her visitor up and down admiringly. "You really *don't* have 'that sort of problem,' do you?"

Sir Ethan elected to ignore this interruption. "The last one — six months ago, that was — was long and difficult. The baby was 'ealthy, but I almost lost me wife."

"And what does this have to do with me?"

Sir Ethan took a deep breath. "I thought there must be a way — it stands to reason — if there weren't, you'd 'ave at least two or three —"

At this point Sir Ethan's speech became so disjointed as to render it incomprehensible. Mrs. Hutchins, however, was as compassionate as she was astute, and decided to take pity on her stammering guest.

"Come now, Sir Ethan, we are business people, you and I," she said bracingly. "You want me to tell you if there is a way for you to bed your wife without risking a potentially fatal pregnancy. In fact, you want to eat your cake and have it, too."

Sir Ethan winced at her blunt speaking, but answered with equal candor. "Aye, that I do."

"Furthermore, you suspect that there *is* such a way, and that I must know of it — else, as you so eloquently observed, women in my profession would have a house full of children."

His expectant silence gave Mrs. Hutchins to understand that her assumptions were correct.

"Your best bet, Sir Ethan, would be to take your pleasure elsewhere. I am free this afternoon, if you would like to come upstairs." She rose and held out one hand invitingly.

Sir Ethan shook his head. "No, that won't do."

"Pray, why not?"

"Because I love me wife," he said simply. "No offense, madam, but I don't want any other woman. If there's no other way, I'll —"

"Yes?" she prompted. "What *will* you do?"

Sir Ethan gave a rueful smile. "I'll take plenty of cold baths."

Mrs. Hutchins had been seventeen years in her profession, and in that time she thought she had seen it all. She had been wrong. This married father of four somehow seemed as innocent as the greenest youth bedding his first woman. She would gladly have foregone her usual exorbitant fee and taken him upstairs for free, just for the novelty. But he would not have gone with her if she had offered, and somehow she would have been disappointed in him if he had.

"Very well, Sir Ethan. Your assumptions are correct. There is such a way as you supposed. But I am in business to earn a living, you know. How much are you prepared to pay for the information you seek?"

The sum he proposed made her blink. "My dear sir, if all men valued their wives so highly, I should soon be forced to seek another profession."

She rang for tea and cakes, and instructed her butler to deny her to callers. Then she and Sir Ethan spent a very informative half-hour, at the end of which time he took his leave. His hostess did not ring for the butler, but instead walked him to the door herself.

"Remember, Sir Ethan, if your wife objects, you may always be sure of a welcome here."

"Thank you, madam," he answered in a tone which, while respectfully polite, clearly communicated to her the unlikelihood of his ever appearing on her doorstep again.

"Oh, and Sir Ethan —"

He had already started for the stair, but upon hearing her call his name, he turned back, and found himself seized by the lapels and kissed squarely on the mouth with a ferocity which knocked the curly-brimmed beaver from his head.

"Forgive me, ducky," she said with a wink, when at last she released him, "but I do have a certain reputation to uphold."

❦

Lady Helen shifted to the edge of her seat as the carriage clattered down the familiar London streets. Very soon now she would be reunited with her husband and (she devoutly hoped) all her fears would be put to rest. For there was no denying that, in his absence, her doubts about her marriage had fed upon themselves until she no longer knew what to believe. At times, such as when a hastily scrawled letter had been delivered assuring her of his safe arrival in the Metropolis, she chided herself for her own foolishness; at others, primarily when she lay alone in her bed at night, it was all too easy to believe that he had never truly loved her at all, that winning her hand had been nothing more than a challenge to him, another rung on the ladder from workhouse orphan to knight of the realm.

In the light of day, she knew these fears to be exaggerated to the point of absurdity. Still, nothing less than the sight of his face and the feel of his arms about her would put the problem (for problem there undeniably was) in its proper perspective. Consequently, her heart leaped every time she sighted a carelessly dressed, dark-haired man of medium height — no very rare breed in London, and hence the source of considerable agitation of spirits. The nearer they came to her Grosvenor Square town house, the more impatient Lady Helen became. The excited chatter of Miss Colling, so infectious at the beginning of the journey, had begun to pall. Lady Helen could only be thankful that the twins, at least, had long since fallen asleep, and that the younger children were riding with Nurse in a separate carriage some distance behind.

"*Voyons!*" cried Lisette. "Why do we go so slowly?"

"I don't know," Lady Helen confessed.

"Have we indeed slowed down? I thought as much, but supposed it must be my imagination."

As if in confirmation, the carriage rolled slowly to a stop. Lady Helen rapped on the panel overhead. It opened on the instant, and the coachman peered down at his passengers.

"Yes, my lady?"

"What is the matter, Dixon?"

"Looks like a farm cart's met with an accident up ahead. There's turnips all over the road."

Lady Helen made an impatient noise, to which the coachman was quick to respond. "Shall I make a detour, ma'am?"

"Yes, please."

The overhead panel closed, and the carriage inched forward until it reached the intersecting street. The coachman swung the carriage off the main thoroughfare and onto a narrower residential lane. Progress along this street was of necessity slower, but it was still progress of a sort. Lady Helen sank back in her seat and strove to bear with patience the little bit that remained of the long journey. As the carriage turned onto Green Street, however, she sat up abruptly. The door of a pleasant house had swung open, and on the threshold there appeared a carelessly dressed, dark-haired man of medium height, bidding farewell to a stunning titian-haired woman. Lady Helen silently chided herself for her own foolishness. What would her husband be doing in Green Street, of all places, where resided some of the most notorious courtesans in England, including the Duke of York's mistress, Mary Ann Clarke, and Lord Waverly's erstwhile paramour, Sophia Hutchins?

Even as she dismissed the notion, the pair embraced shamelessly upon the front stoop. Lady Helen's first thought was for Lisette, to make sure her young guest was not subjected to a scene of such gross impropriety. Then the hat fell from the man's head, and all other considerations fled from her mind but one: the curly-haired man kissing Sophia Hutchins so passionately was unquestionably, undeniably, her own husband.

For Lady Helen, the remainder of the trip passed in a blur. A strange buzzing noise filled her head, almost drowning out the lilt of Lisette's French accent as she chattered cheerfully, unaware that her hostess's world had just come to an end. After what seemed to Lady Helen like an eternity, the carriage drew to a halt in front of 23 Grosvenor Square and the door was opened. At the sight of the footman waiting to hand her down, however, twenty-five years of training came to the fore. Smiling serenely, she placed her hand on his proffered arm and inquired into the health of his widowed mother as she stepped lightly down.

Once inside, Lady Helen flung herself with a passion into the details of house-wifery, seeing her children settled in the nursery and the best guest chamber prepared for Lisette, conferring with the housekeeper and the cook, and seeing to the bestowal of her muslins and silks in the clothes-press. In this manner she contrived to keep herself busy for some time until Sir Ethan, returning home late after dining at his club, was informed by the butler that Lady Helen was now in residence, having arrived that very afternoon, a full three days earlier than anticipated.

" 'as she, now?" he asked with every appearance of pleasure, surrendering his hat and gloves to Evers's care. "I wish you'd sent a message to me at Brooks's. I'd've been 'ome sooner."

"I'm very sorry, sir. I should not have wished to bother you."

"No bother at all," his master assured

him. "But never mind. I'll go up at once."

As if in proof of this statement, he took the stairs two at a time. He found his wife in her bedchamber, wearing a lace-trimmed dressing gown and arranging her combs and brushes on an elegantly carved rosewood dressing table. These had already been put to good use, for Lady Helen's honey-blond hair was unpinned and tied with a ribbon at the nape of her neck.

" 'elen, me love!" he said, gazing at her in a manner evocative of a starving man invited to a Carlton House banquet.

A silver-backed brush slipped from Lady Helen's hand and clattered to the table. She was not ready. She had not yet decided what she would say to this man she had thought she knew so well. When he had not come home for dinner, she had assumed she would not see him until morning, and she found it grossly unfair that she should have to face him now, undressed and with her hair hanging down her back.

"Ethan, darling," she said, smiling through stiff lips. "You are looking well."

"Never better," he declared, crossing the room to take her in his arms. "I didn't think to see you until next week, though.

You took me by surprise."

"Yes, I daresay I did."

He would have kissed her soundly, had she not pulled away after the briefest of pecks. He released her, since she seemed to wish it, but far from leaving the room, he sat down on the edge of the bed and regarded his wife steadily. "I've missed you, 'elen."

She would have reminded him that they had endured separations far longer than this, but something about the look in his eye and the tone of his voice gave her to understand that he was referring not to the previous fortnight, but to a longer period — one approaching six months. The knowledge that he would come to her now, straight from his mistress's arms, made her feel ill.

"It's late, Ethan, and I've still a thousand things to do —"

"Aye, love, I won't press you," he conceded, not without regret. "I've waited this long, I daresay I can wait a bit longer. I trust you 'ad a good journey?"

"Well enough, though rather long," she replied, both relieved and disappointed at his easy capitulation. "There was an accident involving a farm cart and a load of turnips, so we were obliged to make a detour. Down Green Street," she added pointedly.

She might have saved her breath; he had not the grace to look ashamed. "I don't care 'ow you came, just so long as you're 'ere," he said with such conviction that Lady Helen almost believed him. "And the children?"

"They slept much of the way, and Miss Colling was a great help in entertaining them when they were awake."

"She's an 'elp you won't 'ave after today," Sir Ethan told her. "Waverly's purchased a special license. They're to be married tomorrow morning."

"Are they, indeed? It seems a very odd match."

"Aye, that it does. But so did we, love, and just look at us."

"Yes," she said sadly. "Just look at us."

6

We will be married o' Sunday.
WILLIAM SHAKESPEARE,
The Taming of the Shrew

Lord Waverly called for Lisette promptly at nine o'clock the following morning. She was fetchingly attired for her nuptials in a pink muslin morning dress fashioned for her by Lady Helen's mantua-maker in Manchester, there having been no time to order a wedding gown from that lady's more fashionable London modiste. Her ravaged curls were hidden — and her heart-shaped face charmingly framed — by a deep-brimmed bonnet trimmed with pink roses. She looked absurdly young, and Waverly wondered anew at the vagaries of Fate in contriving such an ill-assorted union.

He did not voice these reflections to his bride, however, but handed her up into his curricle, climbed up beside her, and set the horses' heads toward St. George's,

Hanover Square. They had gone some distance in silence when Lord Waverly, glancing at his bride and seeing naught but the brim of her bonnet covering her downcast face, asked, "Are you frightened, Lisette?"

"*Mais non,*" she replied without looking up. "I am not frightened, milord."

"Nervous, perhaps?"

"Perhaps a little," she confessed. "After all, one does not get married every day."

Having been aggressively pursued by damsels eager to hear themselves addressed as "my lady," he found her reluctance less than flattering. "I'll not eat you, you know."

"*Oui,* I know," she said sadly.

Having arrived at the church, he drew the vehicle to a halt and leaped down. He tossed a coin to a nearby lad, promising the boy another one for walking the horses until his return, then turned to hand Lisette down. Tucking her hand into the crook of his elbow, he escorted her up the stairs, past a flower woman selling her wares on the church steps. Obeying a sudden impulse, he purchased a posy of violets from her basket and presented these to his bride.

"*Merci,* milord," Lisette whispered,

smiling shyly up at him.

The wedding ceremony was simple and brief. There was no wedding breakfast, nor were there any guests, unless one could count the few pious souls who had arrived early for Sunday services. The bishop peered suspiciously at the youthful bride, then pushed his spectacles higher onto the bridge of his nose and re-examined the special license. Apparently convinced that all was in order, he read the service from the Book of Common Prayer, asking the pertinent questions and nodding benignly as the earl and Lisette made the appropriate responses. The transaction was completed in less than fifteen minutes.

Afterwards, Lord Waverly escorted his lady back up the aisle, but upon seeing the church now half-filled with worshippers, the new Lady Waverly hung back.

"Should we not stay for services, milord?"

"Me, attend church?" drawled Waverly. "My dear child, the roof might cave in."

"*Vraiment?*" asked Lisette, gazing curiously at the carved ceiling over her head. "It looks strong enough."

"I meant," the earl explained with exaggerated patience, "that I have not been in the habit of regular attendance."

Lisette saw nothing to wonder at in this declaration. "*Naturellement!* You have been in France."

"The omission is not a recent one, I fear."

"Ah! Then no doubt *le bon Dieu* will be pleased to see you again," said Lisette, undaunted.

Lord Waverly, conceding defeat, made no further protests, but ushered his bride to a nearby pew. As the service progressed, the earl might have been pleased to note that the roof remained intact; however, he had little thought to spare for this circumstance, his mind being occupied with more pressing concerns. From the moment he seated himself beside Lisette, he was aware that they were the objects of considerable interest. As the bishop delivered his sermon, the earl became increasingly cognizant of the surreptitious glances being cast in their direction — glances containing every known emotion from scandalized amusement to speechless outrage. Even he, who was well aware of his tarnished reputation among the *ton,* was a bit taken aback by the violent reactions his presence seemed to provoke.

All was revealed, however, at the conclusion of the service. No sooner had Lord

Waverly escorted his bride from the church than Lady Worthington, once a bosom-bow of the earl's late mother, descended upon him, righteous anger evident in the quivering ostrich plumes of her bonnet and the swell of her formidable bosom.

"I had heard you were returned to Town, Waverly, but I could scarcely credit it," she began in a voice well-suited to the bosom that sustained it.

"For once, my lady, rumor did not lie," Waverly replied, bowing over her hand.

"Would that it had! For it is obvious your sojourn abroad has done nothing to improve your delicacy of mind. Mark my words, Waverly, this time you have gone too far! Desecrating a holy place by bringing your doxy here —"

Tight-lipped, the earl drew his wide-eyed young countess forward. "Madam," he addressed Lady Worthington, "may I present to you my wife, Lady Waverly?"

"Your — *wife*, you say?"

In an instant, Lady Worthington was all graciousness, bowing to Lisette as if she were visiting royalty. The crowd which had gathered to witness the confrontation now quickly dispersed to spread the news of Waverly's shocking return to Town with a wife in tow, leaving the earl to reflect upon his own mishandling of the situation. He should, he now realized, have inserted an announcement in *The Morning Post* to preclude just such a disaster. As matters now stood, he only hoped Lisette's English was not sufficient for her to understand the insult she had just been dealt. He retrieved his equipage from the boy in whose charge he had left it, and bundled Lisette aboard before her presence provoked an even more scandalous confrontation.

It was not until they had left the church and its inquisitive parishioners behind that the earl began to breathe easier. Alas, even then his relief was premature, for they had not yet reached Oxford Street when a whimsical high-perch phaeton in the form of a seashell drew abreast of them. At the sight of this curious vehicle and its driver, Lisette leaned forward for a better look.

"Ah, milord!" she cried. "Who is *that?*"

Waverly turned to inspect the dashing equipage and beheld its occupant, a handsome red-haired woman of about his own age, leaning against the green velvet squabs. Perceiving his sudden interest, she smiled coyly and rearranged her well-endowed form in a more advantageous posture.

" 'That,' as you put it, is no one who need concern you," Waverly said dampingly.

"But she knows you," Lisette insisted. "She waved at you ever so slightly and I think, *oui,* I am almost certain that she winked."

"No doubt she did. But just because *I* am acquainted with a particular person does not mean I wish my wife to make that person's acquaintance."

"And this woman, she is such a person?"

"She is."

Lisette pondered this revelation for a long moment. "She must be a very wicked woman, *n'est-ce pas?*"

"Very."

"Is she one of your *chères amies?*"

"If you will recall," said Lord Waverly through clenched teeth, "I have been living in Paris for the last four years. If she *had* been my *chère amie,* you may be sure we have long since forgotten the connection."

"*You* may have forgotten, perhaps, but *she* has not. She did wink, you know."

Lord Waverly strove with himself. "Lisette, whatever my numerous faults, I have never attempted to deceive you as to my character. I have had numerous agreeable connections with ladies of dubious virtue, and I will no doubt do so again in the future. One of these, as you have surmised, was Mrs. Sophia Hutchins. However, she is not now my mistress, nor do I expect her to resume that position. Furthermore, if and when I do choose to establish such an arrangement with another woman, I can assure you it will be conducted discreetly, and in such a way as to spare you any embarrassment. In return, I shall expect you to turn a blind eye to females of this sort, not ogle them in the streets!"

"*Oui,* milord," murmured Lisette, eyes once again fixed on the posy in her lap.

"And of course," he continued more gently, "I shall make every effort to grant you an equal amount of freedom. You may have whatever friends you choose, and although we have not yet had time to discuss marriage settlements, you shall have sufficient pin money for your needs. Until then, you may have your bills sent to me for payment."

"Pin money?" echoed Lisette, brow wrinkling at the unfamiliar term.

"Discretionary funds to spend as you see fit."

Lisette's eyes sparkled with sudden interest. "And I can buy with this 'pin money' anything I like?"

"Anything," declared Lord Waverly, thankful to have the conversation turned to a more seemly topic.

When the curricle at last rolled to a stop before Lord Waverly's sketchily refurbished Park Lane town house (which had been spared from foreclosure only by virtue of its being entailed), the earl ushered his countess into her new home, introduced her to its senior staff, surrendered her to the housekeeper for a brief tour, and promptly set out for White's. This cavalier treatment was not lost on his bride, but as her fertile brain had begun to form a plan, his absence suited her purposes very well.

It was obvious to the meanest intelligence that her new husband had a marked preference for wicked women; therefore, she determined, a wicked woman he should have. She had no very clear idea how to achieve this admirable goal, but the chance encounter with *Madame* Hutchins had at least shown her a reasonable place to start. Lisette's understanding of the English monetary system was rudimentary, but she was reasonably certain that the pin money of which the earl had spoken was insufficient for the purchase of an equipage such as *Madame* had driven. However, that lady's kohl-rimmed eyes and rouged lips should not be beyond Lisette's means to reproduce. With this end in view, she made discreet inquiries of the housekeeper, and set out for Piccadilly and the new Burlington Arcade, a veritable cornucopia of shops where, the housekeeper assured her, a lady might find anything she desired in the way of beauty aids.

She wandered among these for some time, wishing she knew if the unspecified pin money would stretch to cover this branch of artificial roses, or that length of ribbon. Until she could be sure, she felt it was best to restrict her purchases. And so, with a small sigh of regret, she laid aside a pretty painted fan and selected instead a small pot of kohl and a somewhat larger one of rouge. These she gave to the shop's proprietor, along with instructions as to remuneration.

"You will please to send the bill to Lord Waverly," she said in her lilting accent, as her purchases were wrapped in brown paper.

"*Pardon, mademoiselle,*" interrupted a masculine voice as she bade the shopkeeper farewell. Lisette turned and saw a dark-haired young man doffing his hat in an elegant, if somewhat exaggerated, bow. Even if he had not addressed her in her native tongue, she would have known at a glance that he was French. Small and wiry of build, he displayed the fashionable extravagances of the *Incroyables:* in this case, a pair of billowing Cossack trousers in a salmon color, topped with a green cutaway coat boasting wide lapels. "I perceive from your speech that you are French. May a fellow traveler welcome you to these shores?"

"*Merci, monsieur,*" replied Lisette with a smile, collecting her bundle from the counter before turning away.

"Wait! You will allow your fellow countryman to relieve you of your burden, *oui?*"

Lisette, looking down at a package which might easily have fit inside her reticule, had she thought to provide herself with one, had to laugh. "*Mais non, monsieur,* I would not so trouble you. It is not at all heavy."

"But you will allow me to escort you home," persisted the Frenchman.

"*Merci, monsieur, mais non.*"

"You are too cruel, *mademoiselle!*"

While Lisette could not deny that it was pleasant to be admired by a personable young man, his importunings were beginning to attract an embarrassing degree of attention. Seeing that he might cause a scene if not given some rôle in her return to Park Lane, she offered a compromise.

"You may not escort me home, *monsieur,* but you may call for me, how do you say, a hackney, if you will be so kind."

"You have only to say the word, *mademoiselle,* and Étienne Villiers, he will see that it is done!"

With this declaration, M. Villiers all but hurled himself into the street, calling for a cab with great gusto and much Gallic gesticulation. In no time at all Lisette was settled within, the order was given, and the horses whipped up. Lisette bade farewell to the obliging M. Villiers, and whiled away the short journey in blissful dreams of her husband's surprise and delight when he beheld his bride's transformation.

Alas, it must be said that these fell woefully short of her expectations. When the dinner gong sounded at eight o'clock, Lisette arose from her dressing table and made her way to the drawing room where the earl awaited her. Remembering the behavior of Mrs. Hutchins, Lisette paused just inside the door, flinging her shoulders back and thrusting her small bosom skyward. Her eyelids drooped languorously and her lips were slightly pursed, allowing him to experience the full effect of rouged mouth and kohl-ringed eyes.

"Bon soir," she murmured huskily.

"Good God!" exclaimed Lord Waverly, when he could speak at all.

Much encouraged by this utterance, Lisette closed her eyes in expectation of his passionate embrace. Great, therefore, was her surprise when she found her hand seized in a rough grasp and her person propelled none too gently from the room. She hastily caught up her skirts with her free hand as Waverly started up the stairs, all but dragging her behind. He did not release her until he reached her bedchamber on the floor above. Without a word, he crossed the room to the washstand and poured fresh water from the pitcher into the basin. He withdrew his handkerchief from the breast pocket of his coat, then plunged it into the basin, wrung it out, and, taking Lisette's chin in his hand, very deliberately began to scrub off every trace of her painstakingly applied *toilette*.

Lisette submitted to this procedure meekly enough, only asking, crestfallen, "You do not like it, milord?"

"I think you look like a damned raccoon," he informed her.

112

Lisette's eyes opened wide. "What is a damned raccoon, *s'il vous plaît?*"

"A raccoon is a small forest creature native to America. As for the other, it is a word you must not say."

"Why not?" demanded Lisette.

"Because if you do, the raccoons will nip off your nose," the earl replied without hesitation.

"*C'est absurde!* How can they, if they are in America?"

"Not all of them are there. As a matter of fact, I believe there is one in the menagerie at the Exeter 'Change."

Lisette squirmed eagerly, forgetting for the moment that she was too old — and far too wicked — to take pleasure in such childish pursuits. "I think I would like to see this raccoon. Will you take me, milord?"

"Perhaps, someday — but *not* if you insist upon painting yourself up like a Covent Garden strumpet! Be still now, and close your eyes."

Lisette complied, and Waverly dabbed the last of the black kohl from her eyelids. Her skin glowed from the force of his scrubbing, and Lord Waverly, studying his handiwork, was seized with a sudden urge to kiss her upturned face. Lisette, opening her eyes at just that moment, knew nothing of his inner struggle. She saw only his frowning countenance and ferocious expression.

"I — I am sorry, milord," she stammered. "I thought it would please you."

"I would love to know what I have done to give you such an idiotic notion," replied the earl unsympathetically.

Lisette's remorse vanished in an instant. "You said yourself that I might buy whatever I wished!" she reminded him.

"I spoke no less than the truth. You may certainly buy all the rouge you like; you may not, however, wear it."

"*Bah!*" cried Lisette, stamping her foot in vexation. "*C'est absurde!* What good is it that I should purchase cosmetics if I am not allowed to wear them?"

"What good, indeed?" commiserated the earl, unmoved by this outburst. "I trust you will ask yourself that question next time you visit the Burlington Arcade."

"You are unreasonable, milord!"

He looked down at her in mild surprise. "No, why? Because I prefer my wife's face unadorned?"

Lisette's ire evaporated in an instant, and her luminous eyes grew soft. "Do you?"

"Infinitely."

"I think that is the loveliest thing anyone has ever said to me," she said unsteadily.

"And *I* think you have led too sheltered a life, *ma petite*," he replied. "Come now, let us go downstairs before our dinner grows cold."

Smiling mistily up at him, Lisette placed her hand on his proffered arm, and together they descended to the dining room in perfect charity with one another.

🍎

While the earl and his countess sat down to supper in Park Lane, a short distance away in a hired lodging in Clarges Street, a very different pair sipped their after-dinner port. Upon emptying his glass, one of these, a personable if somewhat foppish young man, reached into his pocket for his snuff box and addressed his companion in French.

"Tell me, Raoul, what think you of this blend? I bought it today at a little shop in the Burlington Arcade."

Raoul pushed the enameled box away petulantly and responded in the same tongue. "I am pleased to know you are amusing yourself so well, prowling about the local shops. Me, I have business to attend to."

"Perhaps you work too hard, *mon ami*.

You should take time for the small pleasures."

Raoul's only reply was a snort of derision.

"And the great joy of these pleasures," continued his companion, unfazed, "comes of their being so many times unexpected. What do the English call it? Serendipity! Yes, that is it. Why, only today I met a young lady —"

"And you call this unexpected? I would be more surprised, Étienne, if you had *not* met a young lady."

"Ah, but this lady, she was French. And so young! Her hair, it was dark, and her eyes —"

Raoul seized him by the sleeve. "You have found my cousin Lisette!"

"Alas, she did not give her name," Étienne admitted mournfully.

"But you know it was she!"

"If the lad we saw in Amiens was indeed your cousin, then it was very probably she."

"Did you follow her?" Raoul asked urgently. "Where did she go? What was she doing?"

"Why, shopping, of course. That is what one does at the Burlington Arcade."

"Squandering her inheritance, no

doubt," Raoul said bitterly.

"*Mais non!* Only purchasing *le maquillage* for her toilette." After a slight pause for dramatic effect, he added, "And this she did not pay for herself, but told the shopkeeper to send the bill to Lord Waverly."

"Waverly? The English aristo in Amiens?"

Étienne nodded. "It would seem likely."

"What did she do next?"

"She would have left, but I detained her. She would not accept my escort, but did allow me the honor of summoning for her a hackney. She instructed the driver to take her to Park Lane. To my infinite regret, I did not catch the number."

"It is not important, at least not yet. It is too fine a neighborhood for a young French girl in a strange city, *n'est-ce pas?* Depend upon it, the aristo has set her up as his *fille de joie.*"

"I feared as much," Étienne said with a heavy sigh. "And so all your plans come to naught."

"*Mais non.*" Raoul, forgetting he had no patience with such mundane matters, reached for his companion's snuffbox and helped himself to a pinch. "I do not begrudge her, *mon ami.* The Englishman will tire of her soon enough, and then she will beg me to make an honest woman of her."

"You would wed a woman who has lost her virtue?"

"*Naturellement*. After all, it is her forty thousand English pounds I wish to marry. As for the rest, it matters not." He picked up the half-empty bottle and refilled the glasses. "Come now, let us drink a toast to my success, and on my wedding day you shall have five thousand English pounds for your able assistance."

Étienne needed no urging. The two men lifted their glasses and drank deeply.

7

So court a mistress, she denies you;
Let her alone, she will court you.
BEN JONSON, *The Forest*

Lady Helen, along with her two closest friends, sat on a bench in Hyde Park, making small talk and watching from a distance as her children cavorted under their nurse's watchful eye. Little Charles clapped his hands in delight as ten-year-old Lord Randall, the son of Lady David Markham by her first husband, sailed a toy boat in the Serpentine. Charles's brother William, not content with such passive amusement, did his utmost to tumble headfirst into the water, and was thwarted in this ambition only through the frequent intervention of his long-suffering nurse. A second nurse, more fortunate in her assignment, pulled the two infant girls along in a perambulator, accompanied by Lady David's infant daughter in the charge of her own nurse.

"You must both promise to visit me as soon as the Season ends," insisted Lady Tabor, who alone of the three ladies had no children as yet, and whose fashionably high-waisted walking dress concealed, at least for the nonce, the slight swell of her abdomen. "Tabor Hall is rather remote, and I shall be starved for company."

"Of course we will come," declared Lady David warmly. "But are you quite certain you will feel up to having all of us at once?"

"Why not? We have the room, and Aubrey might as well learn to accustom himself to the pitter-patter of little feet."

"But not six pairs at once, surely!" Lady David protested laughingly. "Even Lady Helen and Sir Ethan limited themselves to two at a time!"

Lady Helen smiled absently, but made no reply. Polly, Lady Tabor, had once had all Brighton at her feet. Now her life seemed to revolve around her husband and the birth of their first child. *Is that what has happened to me?* Lady Helen wondered. *Have I become too domestic? Has he grown bored with me?*

Somewhere in the distance a clock chimed the hour, and Lady Tabor leaped to her feet, red-gold curls bouncing beneath a fetching gypsy hat. "Oh, is it two o'clock already? I promised to meet Aubrey's mama in half an hour. She has had the Inglewood christening gown sent down, and wants to show it to me. Aubrey wore it, and it means a great deal to her that his child should do so as well. But I must not stand here talking! Do give my best to your husbands, and tell them they are to bring you to Tabor Hall for the summer."

"Give my love to the dowager, and Ethan's as well," Lady Helen said with a mechanical smile as Lady Tabor hurried away.

Lady David Markham waited until their distracted friend was out of earshot, then turned to fix Lady Helen with a knowing look. "What, pray, is troubling you? You have said hardly a word all afternoon, and even when you did, it was obvious your mind was elsewhere. Have people been unkind about Sir Ethan's knighthood? For if they have —"

"No, no," Lady Helen said hastily. "That is, there will always be a few who — but *their* opinions do not trouble me."

"Then what does?"

Lady Helen hesitated for a moment, undecided as to whether or not to air her private pain, before the need to share the burden won out. She took a deep, steadying breath. "Ethan has taken a mistress."

"Nonsense!"

"It is not nonsense, Emily, I assure you! I saw them together. He — he was leaving her house."

"Pray do not jump to conclusions," cautioned Lady David. "There may be some other explanation for his presence there."

"If there is, I should love to hear it!" declared Lady Helen.

"Perhaps he was there on someone else's behalf. I believe it is not unusual, when a man wishes to make an offer of that sort to a woman, to have a third party negotiate the terms. It is quite possible that someone enlisted him in this capacity. After all, no one can question Sir Ethan's business acumen."

"No, indeed! And I daresay Ethan and Mrs. Hutchins were so pleased with the bargain that they elected to seal it with a kiss, right in the middle of Green Street!"

"Oh, dear," said Lady David, somewhat daunted by this revelation. "That does put rather a different complexion on things."

"Believe me, Emily, if there were any other interpretation to put upon what I saw, I would have seized upon it!"

Lady David patted her friend's hand in sympathy. "Try not to mind it so very much. Difficult as it is to understand, men do not seem to feel about these things the same way women do. The fact that a man has a mistress often has very little to do with his feelings for his wife. My first husband, you know, had a marked predilection for opera dancers, even though in all else he was quite devoted to me."

Lady Helen found devotion a poor substitute for love, and did not hesitate to say so.

"Yes, but men appear to take mistresses for reasons that have nothing to do with the tender passion," Lady David pointed out. "The fear of growing old —"

"Old? Ethan?" scoffed Lady Helen. "At two-and-thirty?"

"— The need to demonstrate one's virility —"

"It seems to me that any man who fathers —" Lady Helen, turning pink, broke off in confusion. "Dear me! I forgot what I was going to say!"

Her friend laughed. "You were going to say, and quite rightly, that any man who sires four children in as many years need have no doubts as to his virility! But I shan't tease you."

"Oh, Emily, what shall I do?"

"Speaking from my own experience, it is usually best to turn a blind eye," Lady David advised. "Not very satisfying, I know, but if devotion and affection cannot hold a man, it is unlikely that tears and recriminations will do so. There is really nothing else to do — unless you choose to retaliate by taking a lover of your own," she added, only half in jest.

"I could never do that," declared Lady Helen.

The following morning saw Lady David's precipitous departure from London, her husband having received in the night an urgent missive from his sister-in-law informing him that her husband and his elder brother, the marquess of Cutliffe, had broken his neck in a riding accident. Lord David departed at first light, both to comfort his brother's widow and to assume the duties of the marquisate which would now fall to him, his brother having left no sons. Lady David not unnaturally accompanied him, but the seed she had inadvertently planted was left behind to take root.

❧

Lady Helen had little time to dwell on her sorrows. She and her husband were promised to attend the opera with Lord Waverly and his countess, those two usually combative gentlemen being reluctantly agreed that their appearance, together and apparently on good terms, would serve to scotch any resurgence of gossip concerning Lord Waverly's abrupt departure for the Continent four years previously. Not that Sir Ethan cared what the tabbies might say about the earl — they could, after all, speak no worse than the truth — but he was well aware of his wife's rôle in the affair, and did not wish to have her long-awaited return to Society marred by hints of past scandal.

And so it was that when Lord Waverly ushered Lisette into the box hired for the occasion by Sir Ethan, they found their host and hostess already ensconced there. Lady Helen, resplendent in gold lace and diamonds, quite cast Lisette's white satin and modest décolletage into the shade. But if the young countess was aware of her disadvantage, she was far too interested in her surroundings to give it a second thought. Lisette's wide-eyed gaze swept the cavernous room, taking in scarlet-curtained and gilt-trimmed boxes occupied by ladies in glittering jewels and men in deceptively sober black and white. Her survey came to an abrupt end, however, at the sight of the woman in the shell-shaped carriage. She was holding court in a box on the opposite side of the opera house. Her magnificent titian hair sparkled with emeralds, and her shockingly low-cut gown clung provocatively to long and shapely legs.

"Dampened," muttered Lady Helen at her elbow.

This sounded so much like the word which Lord Waverly had forbidden her to use that Lisette was momentarily taken aback. *"Pardon, madame?"*

"Her petticoats," Lady Helen explained, giving a slight nod in Mrs. Hutchins's direction. "She has dampened them to make her skirts cling. It is supposed to be quite the rage in Paris, is it not? But then, I daresay they hardly discussed such things at the convent."

As if she knew she was under discussion, Mrs. Hutchins chose that moment to glance at their box, her lips curving invitingly. Lady Helen's suspicious gaze shifted to the gentlemen of the party. Unsurprisingly, the earl had raised his quizzing-glass and was ogling his former mistress reminiscently, and as for her husband — yes, he nodded ever so slightly in acknowledgement, a message so subtle it would have gone unnoticed by anyone less intimately acquainted with him, but to a betrayed wife, as unmistakable as if the words had been tattooed upon his forehead.

Sir Ethan, no great lover of opera, soon left the box in search of refreshments, and Lady Helen, seeing Lisette's attention fixed on the drama unfolding on the stage below, seized the opportunity to address Lord Waverly.

"Mrs. Hutchins appears in excellent looks," she remarked in as nonchalant a manner as she could contrive.

Lord Waverly's left eyebrow arched toward his hairline. "What, pray, do you know of Mrs. Hutchins?"

Lady Helen answered the question with one of her own. "How, pray, do men come by the notion that women's silence on certain subjects must denote ignorance? Of course I knew that you were keeping Mrs. Hutchins even while you were paying court to me. And now that you have returned to Town, do you plan to resume the connection?"

"I am flattered by your interest in my affairs, my dear, but no, I do not. I daresay Mrs. Hutchins has found herself a protector far plumper in the pocket than ever I was."

"You are correct," Lady Helen said. "She has."

The bleakness of her tone and the misery in her eyes told him far more than her words ever could. "O-ho! The sainted Sir Ethan has lost his halo, has he? If you cherished hopes that I might cut him out, I fear you are doomed to disappointment. Having sunk her talons into such deep pockets, Sophia Hutchins will not retract them easily. No, if it is revenge you desire, your best bet is to take a lover of your own."

Lady Helen regarded him speculatively. "You once offered your services in that capacity."

Lord Waverly flicked open his enameled snuffbox and availed himself of a generous pinch. "Am I to understand that you have decided to accept that offer?"

"I'm not — that is, I don't —" Lady Helen glanced across the opera house. Mrs. Hutchins's box was empty, the courtesan departed and her court dispersed. Was she even now trysting with Sir Ethan in some secluded anteroom? Lady Helen's chin rose. "Yes," she pronounced decisively. "I have."

❧

Lady Helen's resolution almost failed

her when, on the fateful evening appointed for the rendezvous, her husband entered her chamber through the connecting door from his own bedroom. Upon seeing her applying the finishing touches to a toilette of peacock-colored satin embroidered with gold, he was moved to inquire as to her plans for the evening.

"Surely you haven't forgotten the Lavenham's ball!" chided Lady Helen. "It promises to be the crush of the Season."

Sir Ethan grimaced. "Try as I might, I'll never understand why the prospect of being 'crushed' should appeal to me."

"You don't wish to go?"

"To be honest, me dear, I've made other plans," he confessed, crossing the room to take her in his arms. "But I'll cancel mine, if you'll cancel yours."

"You would?" Lady Helen asked hopefully.

Sir Ethan snapped his fingers in the air. "Like that," he declared, then unwittingly sealed his fate. "T'was only a late supper in Green Street. Nothing that can't wait."

Lady Helen stiffened in his embrace. "So you propose merely to postpone this — supper — to a later date."

"Aye, I suppose so."

"Pray do not trouble yourself on my account," she said, turning away. "Unlike your 'supper,' the Lavenham ball cannot be postponed. He — they will be expecting me, and it would look odd indeed if I failed to put in an appearance."

Sir Ethan, knowing a lost cause when he saw one, did not press her. She had been in London for less than a se'ennight, and already the loving wife of Lancashire was reverting back to the cold Society beauty he had married four years earlier. He did not begrudge her the gaiety of the London Season; this was, after all, the world she was born to, even if it was one he could never fully share. He had never meant to keep her so long absent from it. Indeed, for a time during the first year of their marriage he had believed, perhaps naïvely, that they might be able to enjoy the best of both worlds. Now, however, he was not so sure.

After seeing his wife on her way, he returned to his chamber and donned his own evening dress, then set out for Green Street. Contrary to Lady Helen's assumptions, he did not call on Mrs. Hutchins, but instead presented himself at a house some distance further down the street, which had the distinction of being the London residence of Lord David Markham's political crony Sir Lawrence Latham, with whom Sir Ethan was somewhat acquainted. Upon being ushered into the drawing room, Sir Ethan discovered his host deep in conversation with two earlier arrivals. Although he had occasionally seen Baron Grenville and Earl Grey at Brooks's, he was not well acquainted with them, and their presence at what he had imagined to be an intimate supper came as something of a surprise. Sir Ethan was not easily intimidated by rank — he had, after all, confronted no less a personage than the Duke of Reddington to demand the hand of his daughter in marriage — but he was slightly taken aback by this gathering of the Whig party's leading lights under one roof.

"Ah, Sir Ethan, so pleased you could join us," said Sir Lawrence, coming forward to greet his guest. "Lord Grenville, Lord Grey, allow me to present Sir Ethan Brundy."

After introductions were made and handshakes exchanged, the dinner gong sounded. Sir Lawrence led the way to the dining room where, over turtle soup and turbot with lobster sauce, Sir Ethan's opinion was solicited on several bills currently before Parliament and his replies received with nods of approval, leaving him feeling very much like a schoolboy being praised by his tutors. Not until the covers had been removed and the port brought out did Sir Lawrence reveal the purpose of the gathering.

"You may have heard, Sir Ethan, that the Marquess of Cutliffe was killed in a riding accident," began his host.

"Aye, that I 'ave," agreed Sir Ethan. "I never met 'is lordship, but 'is brother, Lord David Markham, is a good friend."

"And a good man in the House of Commons," Lord Grenville agreed. "But with his brother's death, Lord David assumes the title, and must surrender his seat in the Commons."

"One hopes, of course, that he will remain active in politics by joining us in the Lords," put in Lord Grey.

"I can't imagine 'im not doing so, as soon as 'is brother's affairs are settled," Sir Ethan assured him.

"I trust you are correct. Nevertheless, there remains the problem of his vacated seat."

"We hope to persuade a promising young man to stand for election in Lord David's stead," explained Lord Grenville.

"You'll 'ave an 'ard time finding someone even 'alf as competent," observed Sir Ethan sympathetically.

Three pairs of eyes pinned him with a look. "You underestimate yourself, Sir Ethan."

As comprehension dawned, Sir Ethan set down his glass with a thud. "Did I miss something?"

"I think we understand each other very well," replied his host. "We want you to consider standing for election to the House of Commons — specifically, for the seat soon to be vacated by Lord David Markham."

"And what," asked Sir Ethan slowly, "makes you think I would stand a chance of being elected?"

"I suspect your chances are better than you think," asserted Sir Lawrence. "Only consider, you are in the unique position of being able to attract both the common workers, who will no doubt embrace you as one of their own, and the landed gentry, by virtue of your wife's connections."

Sir Ethan smiled. "As to me wife's people, I wouldn't count on getting any support from that quarter, if I were you. They're all dyed-in-the-wool Tories."

❦

Lord Waverly paced the marble floor at

the foot of the grand staircase, glancing up to check the time on the hall clock. It was already past ten o'clock, and the Lavenham ball had begun over an hour earlier. It was expected to be one of the crushes of the Season, and he and Lady Helen had determined that their brief absence from the festivities would go undetected in such a crowd. Furthermore, the architect who had designed Lavenham House early in the previous century had possessed the foresight to equip the ballroom with any number of conveniently placed alcoves where assignations of an amorous nature might be kept with no one the wiser. Anticipation made him impatient. In less than an hour, he would finally have the woman who had haunted his thoughts for four long years — and at the same time have his revenge upon the man who had humiliated him, the same man to whom he was now, most gallingly, deeply in debt. He glanced at the clock again. Lady Helen would already be there, no doubt wondering what was keeping him.

A movement from above caught the corner of his eye and drew his gaze up the sweep of the great staircase. Lisette, her nose in the air, slowly descended the stairs. She wore the same white satin gown she had worn to the opera — it was, after all, the only evening dress she possessed — but now its demure folds were plastered to her legs, and water dripped from the points of its van-dyked hem.

"Have we had a sudden rainstorm?" Waverly asked this vision in some bemusement.

"I have dampened my skirts," Lisette announced unnecessarily. "I am very daring, *n'est-ce pas?*"

"Indeed you are," the earl agreed. "You risk catching your death of cold."

Lisette's face fell. "*That* is what you think of when you look at me, that I will catch cold?"

"That, and the likelihood that you will ruin the carpet."

"You did not think of colds and carpets last night, when Madame Hutchins wore a gown *so!*"

"No — nor, for that matter, did I think of Mrs. Hutchins at all," said Waverly. *Ah, but could you say the same of Lady Helen Brundy,* an unwelcome voice intruded. In an attempt to drown it out, the earl barked at Lisette, "Go to your room and change your clothes. Do not wait up for me; I shall see you in the morning."

Lisette regarded him with a wounded expression. "You would go without me?"

"My good child, you have nothing else suitable for evening wear," Waverly pointed out in some exasperation. "What would you suggest I do?"

"You could stay home and keep me company," she said coaxingly.

The earl looked away. "Impossible. We have already promised to attend. I will make your excuses to Lady Lavenham."

Having dispatched Lisette to her chamber, Waverly set out on foot for Lavenham House, but the episode was sufficient to destroy his anticipation for the approaching rendezvous. He had, he reminded himself, no reason at all to feel guilty. He had never promised Lisette that he would be faithful to her; in fact, quite the reverse: he had been brutally honest with her regarding his past behavior, assuring her that, while she could rely upon his discretion, she had best not look for fidelity. Indeed, he was probably wise to take a lover at once, lest Lisette note his abstinence and develop unrealistic expectations. Yes, he would establish an amorous connection with Lady Helen, at least until — until what? Until they tired of the game, he supposed, or until Ethan Brundy discovered the arrangement and dragged

136

his errant wife back to Lancashire, rendering it necessary for him to establish a new inamorata. That, he reflected bitterly, was the trouble with marriage: it made the simplest things so damnably complicated!

In his present state of mind, he was hardly surprised when he arrived at the Lavenham's ball only to discover (by dint of a few discreet inquiries) that Lady Helen had already left. Biting back a curse, he danced once with his hostess's homely daughter, escaped to the card room where he won fifty guineas at whist, and took his leave as soon as he could do so without attracting comment.

He returned to his own house to find it dark, save for a branched candelabrum on a side table in the foyer. He was aware of a pang of disappointment. Had he, perhaps, expected Lisette to wait up for him after all? How deucedly awkward that would have been, to find one's wife awaiting one's return from trysting with another woman — never mind how unsatisfactorily that proposed tryst had turned out. Picking up the candelabrum, he mounted the stairs to his bedchamber.

Upon reaching the second-floor corridor, however, he paused for a moment outside Lisette's door. He turned the knob and opened the door, lifting the candelabrum to illuminate the darkened interior. The bed curtains were drawn back, revealing a slumbering Lisette swathed in crisp linen sheets. Her cropped and tumbled curls surrounded her head like a halo, and he thought what a waste it would have been, hiding them forever beneath a nun's wimple.

Tearing his gaze away, he surveyed the room. A smile tugged at his lips at the sight of the saturated evening gown draped over a towel-covered chair, drying before the smoldering fire. He hoped he had not been unduly harsh with his young wife. Perhaps he should take her to the Exeter Exchange upon the morrow, just to show her he bore her no ill will; she had, as he recalled, expressed an interest in seeing the "damned raccoon" she had so nearly resembled. He made a mental note to keep her away from the duck pond, lest she have any more ideas about dampening her petticoats. Softly, so as not to wake her, he stepped back into the corridor and closed the door.

8

She is a winsome wee thing . . .
This sweet wee wife o' mine.
ROBERT BURNS,
My Wife's a Winsome Wee Thing

The following morning, Sir Ethan and Lady Helen visited the Exeter Exchange, their twin sons having expressed somewhat vociferously an interest in seeing the animals housed in the menagerie. Alas, the outing could not be considered an unqualified success. Although she kept her hand tucked within the crook of her husband's arm as they strolled past the various cages, Lady Helen's manner was distant, and her responses to her children's effusions rather mechanical. Sir Ethan, for his part, was equally preoccupied. As recently as a fortnight earlier, he would have confided in his wife and solicited her opinion, but in view of her current aloofness, the timing hardly seemed appropriate.

In fact, he was not sorry when they encountered Lord Waverly and his countess, and the two parties blended into one. Lisette and the children greeted each other as old friends, and one dragged the others (it was not immediately apparent just who was dragging whom) off in search of raccoons. It said much for Sir Ethan's state of mind that he did not object when Lord Waverly fell into step beside Lady Helen, and the two soon fell behind, allowing Sir Ethan to ponder his situation in relative privacy. He might have been less pleased, however, had he been privy to their conversation.

"Where were you?" Lady Helen chided, speaking softly lest her husband should hear. "I waited at the Lavenhams' as long as I dared, but you never came."

"Domestic difficulties," replied Waverly, adding by way of explanation, "Lisette decided to dampen her petticoats. I daresay the carpet still squishes when one sets foot on it."

"Oh, dear! Whatever possessed her to do such a thing?"

Lord Waverly's left eyebrow rose. "Can you doubt it? You did, of course."

"*I?* I never told her to do any such thing!"

"My dear Helen, no one need *tell* Lisette anything. One has only to put the idea into her head — which, I understand, you did by pointing Sophia Hutchins out to her."

"Did I, indeed? If that was the case, I am sorry."

"No harm done," Waverly assured her, "only a slight delay. Tell me, do you plan to attend the Warrington musicale tomorrow evening? No convenient alcoves, alas, but while the guests are congregating in the music room, it should not be difficult to slip away to one of the bedchambers upstairs."

Bedchambers? Somehow Lady Helen had not thought of the assignation in such bald terms. A vaguely defined rendezvous in a velvet-curtained alcove was one thing; an emulation of the marital act with a man other than one's husband was quite another. Still, the featured performer at the musicale was to be an Italian soprano of the type Sir Ethan particularly disliked. She need have no fear of his accompanying her, even if he had not already made plans to spend the evening in Green Street. "Supper," indeed! She could hazard a guess at what had been on the menu!

"I shall be there," she said resolutely.

Further discussion was rendered impossible as the three elder members of the party drew abreast of the three junior, who were peering into a cage containing, according to a small nameplate attached to the front of the cage, *Procyon lotor*, or common American raccoon. Heedless of the damage to her muslin walking dress, Lisette knelt beside the brothers Brundy, examining with great interest the funny, furry creature twitching its ringed tail as it stared back at her, its bright, inquisitive eyes framed by a band of black fur resembling a mask.

"Oh!" cried Lisette, spying her lord's approach. "*This* is what you say I look like? But this is not like me at all!"

"On the contrary," replied Lord Waverly. "The resemblance is even more marked than I imagined."

"*Pas du tout!* But I think you are teasing me, *oui?*"

"What makes you think so?" asked Lord Waverly, extending a hand to raise his wife to her feet. Lisette reached up to take it, and Lady Helen, observing her laughing countenance and the smile lurking in Waverly's eyes, was somewhat taken aback to find the earl and his young countess on such excellent terms. For the first time, it occurred to her that she and Lord Waverly were serving Lisette a very ill turn. On the other hand, she reflected, glancing at her oblivious husband, perhaps it was better for Lisette to discover the realities of a *ton* marriage early in her wedded life than to suffer a broken heart four years later.

❦

That afternoon, Lord Waverly received a visitor sent to him from the Employment Registry. This person, a middle-aged woman of stern visage (whose austere countenance, had the earl but known it, concealed a most tender heart), he bade be seated on a straight-backed and decidedly uncomfortable-looking chair.

"And your name is — ?"

"Winters, my lord."

"Your previous employer?"

"Lady Braxleigh."

"And the reason for your termination?"

"Death, my lord."

Cold blue eyes regarded her from underneath drooping eyelids. "Your employer's, or your own?"

Winters, undeceived by the earl's lazy mien, remained unfazed. "Lady Braxleigh's, my lord. Had it been my own demise, I should, of course, have given two weeks' notice."

Waverly gave a grunt, which Winters

correctly interpreted as an expression of satisfaction. "I trust they told you at the Employment Registry why you were being sent."

"I was told you had need of a lady's maid, my lord."

"That much is true, but it tells only part of the story. I require an abigail to serve a very young lady. Since attaining sufficient age to be presented to Society, she has been rather, er, cloistered, and thus has no idea how to go on. I will, of course, teach her as best I can, but she will require a woman who can guide her taste in matters of dress."

Winters inclined her head. "I see. Am I to understand this young lady is your daughter?"

The frosty look leveled at her would have quelled a lesser female. "She is my wife."

"I beg your pardon, my lord."

"No need," he said, waving away her apology. "An honest mistake, as it happens."

As if on cue, the door opened at that moment and Lisette entered the room in a swirl of primrose muslin.

"Ah! *Mille pardons,* milord. I thought you were alone."

"Lisette, this is Winters. She is to serve as your dresser."

"My lady," said that woman, bobbing a curtsy.

"Bonjour," Lisette responded, offering her hand. "I am pleased to — *achoo!*"

"Bless you," Waverly responded. "Perhaps you had best go to your room and fetch a shawl."

"But I have not at all the cold," Lisette protested.

"Nevertheless, we should not want you to take a chill after last night's, er, sudden rainstorm."

"Très bien! I will go at once," said Lisette, and tripped lightly from the room.

"That charming child is Lady Waverly?" exclaimed Winters, after the door had closed behind her. "She is enchanting! Men will fall at her feet."

"I had much rather they did not," said the earl dampeningly.

"Unless you would have me put a bag over her head, my lord," rejoined Winters, "I should like to see you try and stop them."

❦

Alas, Waverly's expectations proved to be well founded. Lisette continued to sneeze throughout the day, and her nose acquired a distinctly ruddy hue. Late that night, she rose somewhat unsteadily from her bed and padded barefoot into Lord Waverly's bedchamber.

"I am sorry to wake you, milord," she rasped, "but I fear I have after all *la grippe*."

Waverly awoke with a start, and fumbled for the flint and candle on his bedside table. Once lit, the feeble light revealed Lisette's flushed cheeks and feverishly bright eyes.

"My poor child!" exclaimed the earl. "You should be in bed."

He lingered only long enough to shrug on a frogged dressing gown before scooping up his countess (noting as he did so the unnatural warmth of her skin) and bearing her off to her bedchamber. After tucking her securely beneath the covers and stoking the fire smoldering in the grate, he rang for Winters and instructed her to procure a hot brick for her mistress's bed, and to have the housekeeper prepare a saline draught. He then prevented her from carrying out either of these tasks by delivering a scathing condemnation of her neglect of her ladyship's health, which he apparently expected her to have divined through some form of mental communication. To her credit, Winters neither denied his accusations nor turned in her notice. In fact, the sight of her employer tending to his young wife ("fussing over her like a hen with one chick," she later confided to the housekeeper) planted a certain idea in her mind, one which raised the earl considerably in her estimation.

At first light, Waverly sent for a physician, who examined Lisette and sentenced her to spend the day in bed with nothing to eat but a little weak broth and a vile-smelling potion in a dark brown bottle which, he assured her, would soon have her feeling very much more the thing. One sip of this concoction was enough to make Lisette wrinkle her nose in distaste but, just as the doctor predicted, by evening her fever was gone and she felt sufficiently recovered to be bored with her confinement. Lord Waverly, stopping to check in on her before departing for the Warrington musicale, was made privy to the information that he was a cruel beast to go sauntering forth for an evening of pleasure while she was locked in her room without so much as a book to bear her company.

"Locked?" echoed Waverly in tones of shocked revulsion. "Surely not!"

"Well, no," Lisette was forced to admit.

"But I might as well be, for whenever I get up, you or Winters bundle me back off to bed as if I were a child!"

Lord Waverly, recalling the decidedly unchildlike contours of her feverish body in his arms, thought it wisest not to take the bait. "If you desire a book, I shall bring you one from the library. Tell me, do you like gothic novels?"

"No," Lisette said crossly. "That is to say, I like them very well, but I do not want a book."

"What do you want, then?"

A spark of mischief lit her sunken eyes. "Your company?"

Waverly glanced at the clock over the mantel. "I daresay I have time for a hand or two of piquet before I go."

While Lisette wriggled happily into a more upright position, Lord Waverly went in search of a pack of cards. Having run one to earth, he sat down on the edge of the bed, shuffled the cards and invited his wife to cut, then dealt two sets of twelve cards onto the counterpane.

When Winters entered the room two hours later to check on her mistress, she was treated to the spectacle of Lord Waverly, in full evening dress, sitting Indian style on his wife's bed, engaged with her in lively debate over the legality of her last play. At her entrance, the combatants ceased hostilities long enough to glance at the door and identify the intruder.

"I beg your pardon, my lady, I thought you were alone," said Winters. "I was under the impression that his lordship meant to go out this evening."

"Good God!" Waverly, suddenly aware of the lateness of the hour, leaped off the bed. "It is past eleven already!"

"That is all right, Winters, it is time we were done," Lisette assured her, then added with a smug smile, "Milord is angry with me because he is losing."

"If I am angry with you, it is because you cheat," retorted the earl, although the twinkle in his eyes robbed the words of their sting. "It is far too late to — that is, the Warrington's musicale will be almost over by now, so if you would like to play another hand or two, we will."

"I think not," objected Winters. "Her ladyship should be in bed."

"I am already in bed," Lisette pointed out. "I have been in bed all day!"

"Yes, and you are much improved as a result," said the earl. "Winters is quite right. It is wicked of me to keep you up so late."

Smiling at Lisette's huff of annoyance,

Waverly plumped her pillows and drew the counterpane up to her chin. Then, obeying a sudden impulse, he bent and dropped a chaste kiss onto her forehead. As he bade her goodnight, he made the surprising discovery that, although the last two hours were by no means the wickedest he had ever spent in a lady's bed, they nevertheless ranked among the most enjoyable.

❧

The next morning saw Lisette sufficiently recovered to receive callers, the most significant of whom was Étienne Villiers. This worthy arrived promptly at two o'clock with a posy of flowers with which he hoped, he said, to speed Lady Waverly's return to good health. In point of fact, he had not known prior to arriving in Park Lane that she had been ill; nor, for that matter, had he known that she was Lady Waverly until his comrade, Raoul, had read the announcement in *The Morning Post*.

"*Imbécile!*" had cried Raoul, never in the sunniest of temperaments before breakfast. "She is not his *fille de joie* at all! She is his wife!"

Étienne clicked his tongue sympathetically. "*Alors,* it appears you will not have your forty thousand pounds after all."

"Perhaps," Raoul said thoughtfully, drumming his fingers on the table. "Or perhaps there is still a way."

Raoul had not seen fit to inform Étienne of his plans, but he had beseeched his henchman to try and remember if he had said anything to imply that Lisette had abandoned her convent for a sisterhood of quite another sort.

"*Mais non,* of this I am certain," Étienne stated emphatically. "It was not until I overheard her instructing the clerk to send the bill to Lord Waverly that I suspected that she was no longer a respectable female."

"And what, pray, would a respectable female have been doing jaunting about Amiens in breeches? But never mind that," Raoul amended hastily, lest Étienne be distracted by trivialities. "We must make certain we — you, that is — have not offended her in any way."

Hence Étienne's presence in Park Lane. It was at first his intention to call on the pretext of congratulating his countrywoman on her recent nuptials, but upon hearing the footman who admitted him inquire of the butler whether Lady Waverly's fragile health would permit her to receive visitors, Étienne hastily revised his plans.

He did not think Raoul would object.

"I understand you have been ill," said Étienne, offering his floral tribute. "Now I know why the sun, he refused to show his face yesterday."

Lisette did not for one moment take his extravagant compliments seriously, but she would have been less than female had she not enjoyed hearing them. "You are too kind, *monsieur*. But *la grippe*, she is my own stupid fault."

"*Mais non!* I will not believe it!"

"Still, it is true. I dampened my skirts to make them hang just so, and took the chill. *Alors*, as milord says, I am well and truly punished."

"He must be a monster!" exclaimed Étienne, much shocked.

Lisette's cheeks flushed, but not with fever. "He is *not* a monster! You will not say such things of milord!"

"*Mille pardons!* I meant no offense," Étienne said hastily, eager to correct an obvious misstep. "I meant only that such a delicate flower as yourself should be cherished, not scolded."

Lisette could find no fault with this sentiment, and so Étienne soon coaxed his way back into her good graces. By the time Lord Waverly returned from his club some ten minutes later, they were apparently on excellent terms, as the earl noted to his dissatisfaction when he stopped by the morning room to assure himself that his wife had not taxed her recovery too far. He found her in blooming health, which pleased him, and in lively conversation with a young Frenchman, which did not. He knew his reaction to be unreasonable, and so forbore from making any of the rather biting observations that sprang to his mind. He had, after all, told Lisette that she might choose her friends to please herself; he had not, however, expected her to do so quite this promptly — at least not with friends of the masculine persuasion. And surely she could do better than this foppish puppy! Rather curtly declining an offer of tea, he took himself off to his library for a stiff brandy and a hand of that most inappropriately named of all card games, Patience.

❦

Alas, Lord Waverly's trials were only beginning. He discovered this fact three days later, when he and Lisette were promised to attend a ball at the imposing residence of Lord Langerfield. As this edifice was some few miles removed from Town and possessed the luxury of a small garden in

153

the rear adorned with a Grecian temple, it made an ideal location for intrigues of an amorous nature. It was, therefore, not unnatural that Lord Waverly paced the hall like a caged animal, impatient for his wife to complete her toilette so that they might be on their way.

When at last a slight sound drew his gaze upward, however, all thoughts of Lady Helen Brundy flew from his mind. Descending the staircase was a vision in palest blue, a color Waverly had previously thought flattering only to the angelically fair. He now revised his opinion. Lisette, though clearly no angel, was far more alluring than any heavenly being. A pale blue ribbon had been woven through her cropped curls, banishing forever the image of "Cousin Luc." The hem of her gown was fashionably short, revealing not only her small feet encased in blue kid dancing slippers, but also a pair of neat ankles in white silk stockings. Her *corsage* was more daring than any she had previously worn, exposing the swell of her small, high bosom. Lord Waverly's mouth went dry.

"Milord?" said Lisette, rendered uncomfortable by his close scrutiny and long silence.

When the earl spoke, however, it was not

to his wife, but to her dresser, following at a discreet distance with Lisette's velvet cloak.

"What —" Hearing his voice come out as little more than a squeak, Waverly cleared his throat and tried again. "What have you done to her?"

"I trust I have done what I was hired to do, my lord," Winters said placidly. "Turn her out in a manner befitting her station."

Waverly waved a vague hand in the general vicinity of Lisette's white bosom. "This is hardly suitable for a schoolroom miss!"

"Very true, your lordship, but if you will forgive me for pointing out the obvious, my lady is not a schoolroom miss. She is a countess." Seeing that her employer could not dispute this home truth, she continued. "My lady should, of course, wear jewels, but she has none. Unless, perhaps, there are family pieces kept elsewhere?"

Waverly thought of a particularly fine set of sapphires which had been sold to keep his creditors at bay, and felt a momentary pang of regret for the licentious living which had robbed him of the opportunity to clasp them around Lisette's slender throat.

"No, no family pieces," he said brusquely. "If you're ready, Lisette, we'll be on our way."

9

O! beware, my lord, of jealousy.
WILLIAM SHAKESPEARE, *Othello*

Upon reaching the Langerfield residence, Lord Waverly lingered at his wife's side just long enough to see her provided with a glass of champagne, a plate of lobster patties, and a coterie of young people for companionship before taking himself off in the direction of the card room. To be sure, Waverly reflected, most of these young people appeared to be young men cut from the same cloth as that damned intrusive Frog, but what would you? He had told Lisette she might choose her friends to please herself, and if she took pleasure in the company of a collection of mewlings still wet behind the ears, he would not be the one to say her nay. At any rate, the time still lacked half an hour before he was to meet Lady Helen in the Grecian temple, and he would be damned before he spent it listening to some overdressed coxcomb composing odes to Lisette's eyelashes.

Once inside the card room, he strolled nonchalantly between the tables, dropping a word of greeting here, pausing to watch a player take a particularly neat trick there. At length he allowed himself to be persuaded to join in a game of whist, and when at last the long-case clock chimed the half-hour, he mentally tallied his winnings and found himself several hundred guineas richer. He thought again of the Waverly sapphires, and resolved to make inquiries of his solicitor as to who had purchased them, and whether they might consider selling. Then he tossed in his cards, rose from the table, and sallied forth into the garden in search of Lady Helen.

The Grecian folly, located in the center of the garden, appeared as a pale ghost in the moonlight, its domed roof supported by marble columns. As Lord Waverly drew nearer, one of these detached itself from its fellows and moved forward, eventually resolving itself into the tall slender figure of Lady Helen Brundy.

"So there you are!" she whispered, the plumes on her aigrette bobbing in agitation. "I was beginning to wonder if you had changed your mind."

"Changed my mind?" echoed the earl.

"On the contrary. I have been awaiting this moment for four long years."

Taking her elbow, he guided her up the shallow steps into the shelter of the temple. The brilliant lights from the ballroom did not reach this far, but as Waverly's eyes adjusted to the darkness, he noticed that the folly contained no furnishings save a rug on its smooth marble floor.

"Convenient," he remarked, smoothing the rug with the toe of his evening pump. "One might suppose someone to have been expecting us. Then again, I daresay such structures are often put to such a purpose."

Lady Helen darted a glance at the rug, and licked her lips nervously. "I suppose so."

"Well, then, shall we?" suggested the earl, putting his arm about her waist and drawing her closer.

"Yes, but —" Lady Helen's hands splayed against his chest as if to ward off the very advances which she had herself solicited.

"But what?"

She shook her head. "Nothing. It's only that — well — I've never done this before —"

"Never?" the earl echoed mockingly.

"Surely you do not expect me to believe that your four children were immaculately conceived!"

"Of course not!" said Lady Helen, annoyed. "I meant I have never done such a thing with anyone other than my husband!"

"Four years of fidelity? In that case, your husband is more fortunate than most of the gentlemen of the *ton*. I must remember to congratulate him."

"You will not dare to mention this to him!"

"No? But how can you expect to punish him if he is not to know he is being cuckolded?"

Lady Helen had not previously recognized this flaw in her plan, but she was not prepared to acknowledge as much to the earl. "I did not come here to discuss my husband! Now, if you please, may we just get on with it?"

"Your eagerness overwhelms me, my dear."

Waverly's arms tightened around her and he lowered his head to hers. He could feel her warm breath on his face, could almost taste her lips, when a shriek from the shrubbery nearby made him release Lady Helen so quickly that she nearly tumbled to the floor. He vaulted over the low wall of the folly, then rounded the edge of the ornamental shrubbery just in time to see Lisette struggling in the arms of a rakish young officer in scarlet regimentals.

"*Mais non!* Stop at once, *monsieur,* or I will —"

Her captor only laughed. "You will what? Come, *ma petite,* let us cry friends! Consider it an exercise in diplomacy between your country and mi—"

He got no further before Waverly seized him by the collar. The earl never raised his voice, yet it was as cold — and as lethal — as forged steel. "Your diplomatic skills are superfluous, since the hostilities are long since over. However, the peace could end very quickly, at least as far as you are concerned, unless you unhand my wife and remove your miserable carcass from her presence. Do I make myself clear?"

"Yes, sir — I didn't know — I meant no offense —"

Stammering incoherent apologies, the soldier took his leave, sped on his way by a swift kick to his derriere.

Alone with his wife, Waverly regarded her expectantly. "Well, Lisette?"

"Oh, milord, do not be angry with me! *Vraiment,* I did not know what he meant to do! He asked me if I would like to step into the garden for a breath of fresh air, and as it was very hot inside, I said I would like it very much. But then, when we reached the shrubbery, he tried to — to —"

As Lisette concluded this speech by bursting into a hearty bout of tears, it behooved the earl to gather her in his arms and pat her consolingly. "There, there, child, it's all right."

Lisette looked up, and the tears trembling on her long lashes sparkled in the moonlight. "Then you are not angry?"

"On the contrary. I am extremely angry, but not with you."

"I swear to you, I never did anything to make him think I wanted him to kiss me!"

Waverly stared down at the woman in his arms, at a loss for words. How could he explain to this innocent creature that she didn't have to *do* anything, that she merely had to *be* to have this effect on men? He'd been aware of it since he'd seen her descending the stairs earlier this evening, not dripping wet this time, nor garishly painted with kohl, but looking entirely too grown up — and entirely too desirable — for his peace of mind. What insane notion had possessed him, to assure her that theirs would be a *mariage blanc?* His lip curled in derision as the answer came to him: honor. And just when he had convinced himself that he had none! What a damnably inconvenient time that overrated quality chose to make its presence known! Now he was trapped, living like a monk while he played nursemaid to his young wife, who had no more idea of how to go about in Society than a babe newborn. "Let's step outside for a breath of fresh air," indeed! That one was so old, it had whiskers.

"Milord," Lisette said meekly, interrupting his thoughts, "would you mind very much taking me home now?"

Lord Waverly thought of Lady Helen waiting impatiently for him in the garden folly. God, *yes*, he minded taking her home! He minded very much, indeed. But one look at Lisette's woebegone face informed him that only a cad would abandon her after such an ordeal in order to keep an assignation, and whatever else he might be, he was apparently not a cad. Would that it were so, he thought with a sigh of regret for what might have been. Then, tucking Lisette's gloved hand into the crook of his arm, he led her out of the moonlit garden.

❦

Lady Helen, remaining discreetly out of sight in the Grecian temple, waited for

162

some time before coming to the conclusion that Waverly would not be returning that evening. Stretching her lips in a bright, false smile, she made her solitary way back into the house, where she bade her host and hostess adieu and boarded her carriage for the short drive to Grosvenor Square. The butler was waiting to fling open the door for her, but in spite of his commanding presence, the big house seemed strangely empty.

"Good evening, Evers," she said, her voice echoing in the cavernous hall.

"Good evening, my lady," he replied, relieving her of her velvet evening cloak. "Shall I send for Matthews?"

The last thing she wanted at the moment was to listen to her abigail's chatter. "No, that won't be necessary."

Her footsteps rang on the tiled floor as she made her way toward the curved staircase dominating the far end of the hall. She was perhaps halfway there when a door flew open on her left.

" 'ome so soon, 'elen?"

Lady Helen started guiltily. "Ethan!" she exclaimed, placing one gloved hand over her pounding heart. "How you startled me! I wasn't expecting to see you."

He gave her a searching look. "Nor were

pleased to, I'll be bound."

"What — what nonsense!" she said with a shaky laugh, presenting her cheek for his kiss. "I'm always glad to see you." *At least then I know you're not with that dreadful woman,* she thought.

Sir Ethan, not one to be content with a chaste peck on the cheek, took his wife in his arms and proceeded to do the job properly. For one delicious moment, Lady Helen closed her eyes and relaxed in his embrace, willing herself to forget the Green Street encounter to which she'd been an unwilling witness. But even as she fought to expunge the memory, it came rushing back with startling clarity: her husband, a flame-haired courtesan, and a kiss so ardent it knocked the hat from his head . . .

"Really, Ethan, you're crushing my dress," she protested feebly.

"I 'aven't even got started yet," he informed her with a grin, but his smile faded as she pulled away. " 'elen? What's the matter, love?"

"Why must there be something the matter?" she asked testily. "What if I just want to be left alone?"

"Then I guess I'll leave you alone," he said ruefully, unhanding his wife with

164

some reluctance. "We weren't always like this, 'elen."

"No," she said slowly. "But that was before you started spending all your time in Green Street."

If she had hoped to catch him off guard, she succeeded. She had been so caught up in the gaieties of the Season, he hadn't realized that she was even aware of his meetings with Grenville, Grey, and company, much less that she resented his absence.

"So you know about that, do you?"

Up came Lady Helen's chin, and she regarded her low-born spouse with eight hundred years of ducal forebears invisibly ranged at her back. "Then you do not deny it!"

Sir Ethan shrugged. "What would be the point? I was going to tell you, but you've been gone so often of late, we 'ardly ever see each other."

"So I suppose *I* am to blame!"

"I wouldn't say anyone is to *blame*, exactly," said Sir Ethan, baffled by his wife's response to the prospect of himself sitting in the House of Commons. "I would've told you before, if I'd known it meant that much to you. After all," he added with a smile, "it's 'ardly your area of expertise."

Lady Helen's speechless outrage caused

the plumes on her jeweled aigrette to tremble ominously. After she had risked her life to bear him four children, he had the gall to inform her that she was inadequate! If that were so, he had only himself to blame, for all she knew on the subject she had learned from him! That much, at least, could be remedied: if Lord Waverly had chosen that moment to present himself in Grosvenor Square, she would have commanded him to do the deed at once, without further roundaboutation.

Sir Ethan, seeing that his innocent observation had failed to please, hastened to multiply his sins by adding, "Nor would I expect a lady to interest 'erself in such things."

"How very good of you, to be sure!" retorted Lady Helen, finding her tongue at last. "But if it is truly *my* welfare you have at heart, it seems odd to me that you gave no thought to what must be my chagrin, my humiliation —"

" 'Humiliation,' 'elen?" he echoed incredulously.

"Yes, humiliation! Can you doubt it? To be made an object of ridicule, or worse, pity —"

He didn't hear another word. He could not have been more stunned if she had struck him. She was ashamed of him. He had known, of course, that she had once felt that way. In all fairness, it would have been very odd if she had not, given the vast difference in their stations. But he had thought those days were long gone. In Lancashire, there had been no thought of family trees, no talk of pedigrees. There had been other, infinitely more pleasant, ways to pass the time. But while she considered him good enough to warm the cold North country nights, she was embarrassed to think that the workhouse riffraff she'd married might someday defile the hallowed corridors of power. It was, he supposed, not so very different from the aristocratic ladies who married gentlemen but amused themselves with their footmen — except, in Lady Helen's case, she hadn't the dowry to entice a gentleman, so he had to suffice for both rôles. The funny thing was (or perhaps it was not so funny, now that he thought about it), he hadn't realized until now how badly he had wanted this, how much he had wanted to prove that perhaps he was not so unworthy of her, after all.

"I'd 'oped you would be pleased," he confessed.

"*Pleased?* Pray, what pleasure should I

take in such a state of affairs?"

"At least I'm acting a bit more like a gentleman," he pointed out reasonably. "I doubt you'll find many work'ouse brats there."

In spite of her anger, Lady Helen was touched. Ashamed, too, as she recalled every time she had ever wished her husband spoke, or dressed, or behaved more like a member of her own class.

"Is that what this is all about?" she asked, her voice gentle. "Being more like a gentleman?"

Again Sir Ethan was his own worst enemy. "Only a little," he replied candidly. "I wouldn't even consider it if I didn't already 'ave leanings in that direction."

At this admission, Lady Helen's self-recriminations vanished. "I see. In that case, I suppose there is nothing more to be said."

She turned to leave, but he caught her arm. "Would you rather I didn't, 'elen?"

Oh, how she wanted to say yes! As she looked into his warm brown eyes, it was all she could do not to cast herself on his chest and forgive him everything. But he had not asked for her forgiveness. He had, in fact, not admitted any wrongdoing at all. With such a great gulf between them, what hope did they have for reconciliation? Quickly, before he could see the tears welling in her eyes, she pulled away.

"I'm sure it is a matter of complete indifference to me," she lied, and quitted the room, leaving Evers (still hovering discreetly in the background) to reflect that, had he been the sort to carry tales, he might have dined out on this little scene for a month.

❦

In the reading room at Brooks's club, a glum trio of men assembled before the fire, the low hum of their conversation occasionally increasing in volume sufficiently to cause one or another of the club's members to glare at the three over the top of the *Times* sporting page.

"Damnation!" Lord Grenville exclaimed. "I thought we had convinced him. What can have caused him to change his mind?"

"Surely he must have offered some explanation?" put in Lord Grey.

"He sent a letter by the early post," admitted Sir Lawrence Latham, drawing a folded paper from his breast pocket, "but as to whether it constitutes an explanation, I shall leave it to you to decide."

He unfolded the paper and studied the lines as if seeking some hidden meaning.

"He says he is flattered by our interest, but if he must make a choice, he would rather be a footman than an M.P."

"A footman?" echoed Lord Grey in bewilderment. "I thought the fellow was a weaver!"

As Sir Lawrence refolded the letter, the three men shook their heads at the vagaries of the lower classes.

10

She is herself a dowry.
WILLIAM SHAKESPEARE, *King Lear*

The following morning at eleven o'clock, Mr. Matthew Bartles, senior member of the firm Bartles, Rankin, and Bartles, Solicitors, presented himself in Park Lane and was conducted to the library, where the earl waited to receive him.

"Good morning, Mr. Bartles," said Lord Waverly, gesturing to a chair positioned near the fire. "Do be seated. I trust you were able to obtain an answer to my query?"

Mr. Bartles sketched a bow and seated himself, then withdrew a folded paper from the breast pocket of his coat. "I was, indeed, sir. The Waverly sapphires, a parure consisting of a necklace, tiara, and earrings, were sold for the sum of twelve hundred guineas on 10 July 1816, shortly before you, er —"

"Shortly before I decamped for France," inserted Lord Waverly, regarding with cynical amusement the solicitor's delicately flushed countenance. "You need not spare my sensibilities, Mr. Bartles. Pray continue! Who was the buyer, and is he willing to sell?"

"As to that, my lord, there is a slight complication. The buyer was a gentleman from Lancashire —"

At the mention of that northern county, four years of animosity came rushing to the fore. Lord Waverly gripped the rolled arms of his chair until his knuckles turned white. Damn Ethan Brundy! Which woman now possessed the Waverly family heirlooms — the lady he had once hoped to make his countess, or the most avaricious courtesan in London? He wasn't sure which would be the greater insult. Gradually, however, he became aware of Mr. Bartles's well-modulated voice enunciating words that somehow made no sense.

"— It seems the gentleman went quite mad after becoming estranged from his only son —"

"Nonsense!" interrupted Waverly. "Whatever else may be said of him, I will do him the justice to own that he is quite sane. Furthermore, he has two sons, and neither of them is over three years old!"

His brow puckered in consternation, Mr. Bartles reviewed the papers in his hand. "I assure you, my lord, Colonel Colling fathered one son, John, who died in France —"

Relief flooded Lord Waverly's bosom at the discovery that his family's heritage was not, after all, in the possession of his archrival. Alas, this emotion was short-lived, quickly yielding place to a growing sense of unease.

"Did you say Colling?" the earl asked. "Then the Waverly sapphires were not, in fact, purchased by Ethan Brundy?"

"Why, no. As I said, the buyer was Colonel Robert Colling. Therein lies the difficulty, for Colonel Colling died quite recently."

"Good God!" murmured Lord Waverly.

"The sapphires are now the property of this John Colling's daughter, who inherited everything upon her grandfather's death. I have attempted to contact Miss Colling through the French uncle who is her guardian, but without success."

"And have your attempts to locate Miss Colling extended as far as the *Morning Post*?" inquired the earl with awful courtesy.

"As a matter of fact, they have not, my lord. Why do you ask, if I may be so bold?"

"Because had you consulted the newspaper, you might have read the announcement of my marriage to the lady!" Waverly snapped.

Mr. Bartles blinked at the earl as comprehension dawned. He had been wont to regard his aristocratic client as a wastrel and a rakehell, but now looked at him with new respect. "I see! Pray accept my felicitations upon your marriage, my lord. If I may say so, I should have known you would find a way to salvage your family's heritage."

Lord Waverly bristled at the suggestion that he had married Lisette for her fortune when in fact he had only just now learned of its existence. Still, Lisette's reputation would not be enhanced by his revealing the true circumstances behind the hasty union, so he accepted the solicitor's congratulations and sent the man on his way. Alone in his library, he crossed the room to the window and stared unseeing into the street as he pondered the situation in which he now found himself.

He had married an heiress. Small wonder Lisette's aunt and uncle were so determined that she should wed their son!

Of course, had she entered Saint-Marie, her inheritance would have gone to the convent, but Waverly suspected that Oncle Didier, who practiced law, would have found a way to seize possession for himself.

An heiress. He had known a few heiresses, had even paid half-hearted court to one or two of them. Coy, simpering damsels for the most part, who knew their own worth and made sure no one was allowed to forget it. He did not relish the thought of Lisette becoming one of their number.

As if his thoughts had somehow summoned her, Lisette sailed into the room. She had obviously just arisen from her bed, as evidenced by her tousled curls, as well as the pink silk wrapper covering her night rail.

"Who was here?" she asked without preamble. "I saw someone leaving through my window."

"Leaving through your window?" echoed Waverly in shocked tones. "For shame, Lisette!"

Lisette laughed. "You are teasing me, milord. You know what I mean!"

"I do, and I was. The visitor was only Mr. Bartles, my solicitor, calling on a matter of business. I am sorry if he woke you."

"No matter," said Lisette with a Gallic shrug. "It is very early for business, though."

"It is almost noon," Waverly pointed out.

"Yes, it is very early, as I said." Something in the earl's expression must have betrayed his inner turmoil, for she tilted her head, birdlike, and peered at him more closely. "He did not bring bad news, milord?"

"No, no," Waverly assured her hastily. "Not bad, merely — unexpected."

Taking his reassurances at face value, Lisette banished the solicitor's visit from her mind and claimed his abandoned chair before the fire, drawing up her legs and tucking her bare feet beneath the skirts of her robe. Here she spent the next quarter hour chattering cheerfully to her husband about her plans for the day, until the entrance of the butler with a tray of sherry and cakes recalled to her mind her present state of *déshabille*.

"Oh! I am not dressed!" she cried, leaping to her feet. "I will shock poor Reynolds."

" 'Poor Reynolds,' having been in my family's employ for many years, has seen far worse, I assure you."

Neither Lisette nor Reynolds attempted

to refute this statement, but the countess gave the butler a conspiratorial wink as she departed in a swirl of pink silk. Reynolds, though not so lost to propriety as to return his mistress's wink, could not quite repress the twinkle in his eye, nor the slight twitch of his lips.

Waverly, however, noticed neither of these things, for he was busy cursing himself for a fool. Why the devil hadn't he told her about her unexpected inheritance when he had the chance? He had no real fears about Lisette's new-found wealth going to her head; she hadn't a pretentious bone in her body. Still, there was no denying the fact that with her discovery of her riches would come a subtle change in their marriage. From the day he had helped her escape from Saint-Marie, she had been determined, in spite of his best efforts to set her straight, to see him in the light of a rescuer, a knight in shining armor. He was surprised to discover that he rather enjoyed being adored (although he had no illusions as to his worthiness of adoration), and was loth to give it up. But now it appeared that the single most honorable act of his life — some might argue the *only* honorable act — had been just as self-serving as the most hedonistic episode in a spectacularly hedonistic life. What would happen, he wondered, when Lisette learned that she did not need him nearly so much as he needed her?

And so he said nothing. He knew it was inexcusable, perhaps even cowardly. To say nothing of ironic: he had tried more than once to give her a more accurate rendering of his character, but now that he had the evidence to convince her of the truth of his claims, he was reluctant to use it. Instead, he sent to Colling Manor for the Waverly sapphires which, after a brief interlude at Rundell and Bridge for cleaning, were delivered to Park Lane the following week.

They were promised to attend a ball, and Lisette had been in raptures over the new gown which had been delivered just in time for the occasion. As this costly confection was made of silver net over rich blue satin, it seemed fitting that she should wear the Waverly sapphires. The earl, after putting the finishing touches to his snowy cravat, allowed his valet to assist him into his watered silk waistcoat and form-fitting tailcoat, then picked up the black velvet case from his dressing table and rapped on the door connecting his bedchamber with that of his wife.

"Entrez," called Lisette from within.

Waverly opened the door and found Lisette, resplendent in her new gown, scowling at her reflection in her looking glass.

"I do wish my eyes were blue," she complained to Winters. "Not pale blue, but dark, like lapis."

"I, for one, am glad they are not," rejoined Lord Waverly, stepping into the room, "for these poor things could never compete."

Lisette's face lit up at the sound of his voice, but as she turned to greet him, her gaze fell on the velvet box in his hand. "What is this, milord? *Pour moi?*"

"For you," he said, dismissing the abigail with a glance as he surrendered the case to Lisette.

She opened the box with trembling fingers, and gasped at the riches that lay within. One white hand fluttered to her mouth, then came to rest on the expanse of white bosom revealed by her *décolletage*. "Oh! Oh, but they are too beautiful! I cannot!"

"They are rightfully yours, Lisette." It was the truth, no more and no less.

"But — but you told Winters there were no family jewels!"

"At that time, there were not. They have

belonged to my family since the Restoration. I was obliged to sell them in order to fund my journey to France."

"And now you have bought them back?"

Waverly's smile was curiously lacking in warmth. "In a manner of speaking."

"The cards were very good to you, *oui?*"

"Cards?"

"Or was it dice? However you won the money, you must have been very lucky!"

The earl's expression grew curiously tender, and he stroked his wife's cheek with the back of his index finger. "Far, far luckier than I deserve."

It was a pensive pair who boarded Waverly's crested carriage for the short journey to Dorrington House. Lisette had discovered that, if she closed her eyes and exercised a very little imagination, her cheek still tingled with Lord Waverly's caress. The earl, for his part, was still trying to assimilate his sudden windfall. He knew he should be happy — delighted, even, for living by one's skill at games of chance was a risky occupation at best — but he found he could not quite like the change. Nor could he fully understand the reason for his misliking. To be sure, he had agreed to escort Lisette to England with every expectation of being handsomely rewarded, yet he had offered her marriage with none but the purest of motives. To be paid in coin for his chivalry seemed somehow crass, to say nothing of emasculating: a man liked to think he could provide for his wife, rather than be dependent upon her. It was this, more than anything else, which had made him balk at selling himself to one of those smirking heiresses years ago.

Having arrived at Dorrington House, the earl and his countess allowed a liveried footman to divest them of their cloaks, then joined the receiving line which snaked up the curving staircase. Here Waverly was hailed jovially by an elderly gentleman with frizzled white whiskers.

"Ah, Waverly, good to see you this evening! I trust you'll allow me the chance to win back that monkey I lost to you at White's?"

Wavery bowed. "I am at your service, Colonel."

Lisette looked up at her husband, her eyes sparkling with eagerness. "You won a monkey, milord? Why did you not show him to me? May I keep him for a pet?"

The colonel guffawed. "No, no, my dear Lady Waverly. Merely an expression. Your thieving husband managed to win five hundred pounds from me at whist. 'May I keep him for a pet,' indeed!"

He pinched Lisette's chin in a manner which was more avuncular than lascivious, but which made Lord Waverly yearn to do him an injury, nonetheless. It was, perhaps, a good thing that the butler chose that moment to announce, "Colonel Cyrus Latham," in stentorian tones.

"Meet me in the card room, Waverly, and we'll see if you can win another monkey for your wife," the colonel called, still chuckling, as he moved forward to make his bow to his host and hostess.

Lord Waverly was reluctant to leave Lisette alone, given the turn of events the last time he had done so, but the prospect of a hand of whist for high stakes was too much to resist. Perhaps the transfer of a sizable sum of the Colonel's money to his own coffers would make him feel less of a fortune hunter and more of a man. And so, adjuring his wife to resist any and all attempts to lure her into the gardens, he excused himself to Lisette and made his way to the card room.

Lady Waverly, left to her own devices, felt as if she had been towed out to sea and cut adrift. Everyone seemed to know her as an extension of her once-notorious husband, but her own acquaintances in

London were few. Great, therefore, was her joy when Étienne Villiers solicited her for the Scottish reel about to begin. Conversation was difficult during the boisterous dance, although Lisette managed to disclose to her partner that yes, her husband had indeed escorted her, but was now amusing himself in the card room. It could not be pleasant for him, she said defensively, to return to London only to find that the necessity of squiring his wife to various entertainments prevented him from pursuing his own preferred amusements. By the time the last strains of music died away, Lisette was flushed and breathless from the effort of keeping pace with the lively steps. "You must be quite tired out," Étienne observed solicitously. "Shall we step onto the terrace for a breath of fresh air?"

Lisette's hackles rose. Étienne's attentions, though flattering, had never seemed overtly amorous; yet this suggestion sounded so much like the captain's ploy that she wondered if she had unintentionally encouraged him to think she would welcome more intimate advances.

"*Mais non,* I am quite well," she assured him hastily. "If I may but sit down for a minute —"

"Bien entendu!" exclaimed her countryman. "If you will follow me, Lady Waverly —"

Étienne's ready capitulation banished Lisette's fears to such a degree that she felt quite foolish for entertaining them. "Oh, you must call me Lisette!" she said with a bit more warmth than she otherwise might have done. "For although milord assures me that we are wed, I do not feel at all like a married lady. Does that sound very odd?"

"Not at all," he assured her, deriving a great deal more from this artless confidence, perhaps, than Lisette had intended to reveal. "And you must call me Étienne."

As he spoke, Étienne snagged a bottle of champagne and two glasses from the silver tray of a passing footman. Then, tucking the bottle beneath his arm, he steered Lisette toward a heavy curtain of gold brocade, which he drew back to reveal an alcove furnished with a small table and two chairs artfully arranged before a French window overlooking the terrace.

"But how charming!" Étienne exclaimed. "And see, here is a pack of cards on the table. Shall we try our hand at piquet while you recruit your strength?"

Lisette consented to this scheme at once

and seated herself at the card table. Étienne, taking the seat facing her, filled both the glasses with champagne and passed one across the table to Lisette.

"Now, then, what shall we wager?" he asked as he reached for the cards and began shuffling the pack.

"Wager?" echoed Lisette in some consternation. "I haven't any money."

"Not to worry," Étienne assured her. "You could always stake your necklace."

Lisette's hand flew to the sapphires at her breast. "Ah, but I could not! It is not mine to lose, for it is milord's family heirloom."

Étienne, realizing he had overreached himself, made a quick recovery. "I am sure you underestimate your skill at cards, my lady, but I understand your scruples, and honor you for them. Why not stake that pretty little fan?"

Lisette glanced down at the gouache-on-vellum fan dangling from her wrist by a silken cord. It was indeed a pretty thing, but not terribly valuable. "*Très bien,* but only if you will call me Lisette." Disentangling her hand from the cord, she laid the fan in the center of the table.

"Lisette, then," he said with a smile, adding to the fan a little pile of coins which far exceeded its value.

The pack was cut and the cards dealt, and soon play began in earnest. Alas for Lisette, it was not long before she was obliged to surrender her fan to her opponent.

"But I would not be such a cad as to deny you the chance to win it back," he assured her, replenishing the champagne in her glass.

"I have nothing else to stake," she pointed out.

"Your glove would suffice," suggested Étienne. "I daresay it matters little, for you will have it back soon enough. A man cannot be so fortunate in his cards twice in an evening."

It appeared, however, that Étienne's luck was in that evening, for Lisette's long white glove very quickly went the way of her fan.

"I am fortunate, indeed," Étienne was moved to exclaim as he refilled the glasses. "You very nearly had me, until I drew that queen of clubs."

Lisette, seeing that victory had been so near, was easily persuaded to play again, and had all the felicity of seeing her glove restored to her. So greatly did this please her that she was convinced her luck had turned, and readily agreed to another hand in order to win back her fan. Alas, not only did she lose the glove again, but her other glove soon joined its mate, along with the fan and the little pile of coins, at Étienne's elbow.

"It is probably just as well," she said with a nervous giggle. "I would look very odd wearing only one glove."

"You, look odd? Never!" declared Étienne gallantly. "But if it will make you feel better, I shall stake both gloves on the next hand."

"But I must offer a stake of equal value, and I have no more gloves to wager," Lisette protested.

"If you will permit me," said Étienne, leaning forward to pour the last of the champagne into Lisette's glass, "I have an idea."

❦

Lord Waverly, having lightened Colonel Latham's purse by some two hundred guineas, excused himself from the card room and returned to the ballroom in search of his wife. He raised his quizzing-glass, the better to survey the dancers whirling about the floor in a kaleidescope of color, but the longer he watched, the stronger grew his conviction that Lisette was not one of their number. Training his glass on the French windows opening onto the terrace opposite, he recalled the contretemps of a few evenings previous, and frowned. Despite his words of warning, he had no great faith in Lisette's ability to stay out of trouble. There was nothing for it but to go in search of her. Skirting the ballroom, he reached the French windows, found them unlocked, and stepped out onto the terrace.

The night was clear, and several couples, overheated from the myriad candles illuminating the ballroom, had already sought recourse to the cool night air. However, feminine giggles from the shrubbery gave Waverly to understand the principal attraction here was not the weather. Hearing no sound which might indicate that Lisette (or indeed, any other lady) stood in urgent need of rescue, he turned to return to the ballroom, when a movement from a window some twenty feet away caught his attention.

The curtains were drawn, but the light from within cast sharp silhouettes onto the thin folds. As Waverly watched appreciatively, a lady rose and propped one slender leg on the seat of her chair, then raised her skirt to mid-thigh and fumbled with the garter tied behind her knee. The earl, being a healthy male, raised his quizzing-glass, the better to observe this exercise. Her partner's arm was raised to his head, as if shielding his eyes; Waverly, amused, would have bet all his night's winnings that the man was peeking. At that moment the lady moved her head slightly, and Waverly, still watching through his glass, had no difficulty in recognizing the profile which presented itself to his interested gaze. The short, curly hair, the *retroussé* little nose — they could only belong to one person. He covered the twenty-foot stretch of terrace in less than half a dozen strides, and flung open the French windows with a force that rattled the glass panes.

Just as he had feared, Lisette stood beside her chair, her bare leg gloriously displayed. The earl took no pleasure in the discovery that his wife possessed one of the shapeliest legs he had seen in quite some time. Her opponent, damn his eyes, was the same Frenchman who had so recently haunted the Waverly parlor. The small card table between them contained — besides the card game in progress — an empty champagne bottle and two glasses (one half-filled, the other, Lisette's, empty) and a pile of feminine accoutrements, including a fan, a pair of long kid gloves, two dainty dancing slippers, and one filmy silk stocking.

"What the devil is going on here?" Waverly demanded.

"Why, nothing, nothing at all!" protested Étienne hastily. "Just a friendly game of cards, *oui?*"

"I have played many games of cards, both friendly and otherwise," said the earl, tight-lipped with fury, "but never have I been obliged to remove one article of clothing, nor insisted that my opponent do so."

"I did not *insist* —" Étienne objected feebly, quailing before the earl's thunderous aspect.

"He had no need to," Lisette concurred, swaying slightly on her perch. "For I had to win back my fan, *alors,* then I must win back my glove, and my other glove, and —"

Waverly could hardly hear her words, so distracting was the smooth white length of her leg. "Have the goodness to cover yourself, madam," he said crushingly, then turned back to Étienne. "As for you, you Greeking masher, if I ever catch you sniffing about my wife again, we will settle the matter with pistols at Paddington Green. Do I make myself plain?"

Étienne, perspiration beading on his

forehead, inched his way toward the heavy gold curtain. "Abundantly plain, milord. No harm was intended. I do beg pardon —" Feeling the brocade folds beneath his hand, he plunged through the curtain to the safety of the ballroom beyond.

Alone with his errant wife, Waverly turned to confront her, relieved to discover that while he dealt with Étienne, Lisette had lowered her leg to the floor, allowing the diaphanous folds of her gown to fall about her ankles.

"As for you —"

"I did not go outside with him," Lisette said, blinking owlishly at her livid spouse. "That is what you told me, *oui?*"

"Good God, do I have to tell you everything? One would think you should know not to wager your clothing on the turn of a card! Surely you must have surmised that any man who would suggest such a thing could hardly have honorable intentions!"

"Jusht — just as I must have surmised that the captain invited me onto the balcony with the intention of kissing me?" retorted Lisette. "No, I did *not* surmise! *Vraiment,* I cannot understand why sensible men should act so silly as soon as they find themselves alone with a lady!"

Lord Waverly regarded her with an enigmatic smile playing about his mouth. "Can you not? Then I had best not tell you, lest you think me silly, also."

"But if you do not tell me, milord, how am I to know?"

Waverly looked down at the piquant little face raised so trustingly to his, and became vaguely aware that he was fighting a losing battle. Precisely what that battle was, and why it was so important that he should win it, were not at all clear. He knew only that it would be a relief to give up, at least for a moment, an unequal struggle. Gently, so as not to alarm her, he drew her into his arms and lowered his head to hers. He heard the slight catch of her breath as their lips touched, but the sound was quickly swallowed up as his mouth claimed hers. He could feel the pounding of her heart against his chest, but she made no move to escape from his embrace. At last, the sounds from the ballroom beyond the curtain penetrated his brain, and he slowly released her.

Lisette, raising shaking fingers to her lips, regarded him with wide and luminous eyes. "Oh," she breathed softly.

"That," he said unsteadily, "is why. Now, if you will put on your shoes, I will take you home."

11

Says he, "I am a handsome man,
but I'm a gay deceiver."
GEORGE COLMAN THE YOUNGER,
Love Laughs at Locksmiths

Lord Waverly lingered at the breakfast table long past his usual hour, waiting for Lisette to come down. He did not look for this to be soon, given the amount of champagne she had apparently consumed the night before, but he felt the meeting should not be postponed beyond what was absolutely necessary. It was imperative that Lisette be brought to understand that, one kiss notwithstanding, the nature of their marriage had not changed. He frowned, wondering — not for the first time — what had possessed him to yield to that unfortunate impulse.

He had still not arrived at a satisfactory solution to this puzzle when Lisette entered the sunny yellow-and-white breakfast room, squinting her eyes against the sunlight streaming through the windows.

"Good morning, Lisette." Waverly's greeting was cordial, but not inviting.

"You need not shout, milord," complained Lisette, wincing.

In spite of his best intentions, the earl could not entirely suppress a smile. "I beg your pardon," he said meekly.

Lisette was not deceived. "It is unkind of you to mock me, milord."

Waverly, seeing where his husbandly duty lay, went to the sideboard and poured her a cup of coffee. "Forgive me, but I seem to recall someone assuring me that wine was as mother's milk to the French."

"*Oui*, but I am half English, so I daresay that accounts for it," said Lisette, sipping tentatively at the steaming liquid.

"I am humbled indeed."

Lisette glared at him mutinously. "Say what you will, milord, but I was not nearly so drunk as you were on the day we met, so you cannot scold me!"

"My good child, do not, I beseech you, look to me as your example! I have done a great many things for which I would not only scold you, but probably beat you soundly into the bargain!"

His smile robbed these words of any real threat, but Lisette's expression grew solemn. "I think you were tempted to do so last night, were you not? Pray, milord, what — what did I do?"

Waverly could only stare at her. "You don't remember?"

"No. I know that Étienne was there, and you, and that we were playing cards, but the rest, it is nothing but a blur."

Never had Lord Waverly been so grateful for the debilitating effects of alcohol. And yet, his initial relief at being spared any awkward explanations soon gave way, illogically, to a sense of ill-usage that his kiss had been so easily forgotten. He, at least, had not found it so; instead, he had lain awake for much of the night, trying in vain to find a suitable explanation for his lapse.

"Your memory, such as it is, is accurate, save for one minor detail," said the earl. "Having no coins to wager, you apparently conceived the happy notion of staking various articles of clothing."

Lisette's pale face grew even paler. "Did I — lose very much?" she asked tentatively.

"Suffice it to say that your luck was not in."

Her expressive eyes widened in horror. "Was I — was I *naked?*"

"Good God, no!" Waverly assured her hastily, banishing with an effort the intriguing image her words called to mind. "You were certainly indiscreet, but not indecent."

"Une chance!" said Lisette, somewhat relieved. "There is something else, though — I am embarrassed to ask."

Waverly's voice was gentle. "You need not be."

"Très bien. Did we —" She blushed rosily. "Did you kiss me, milord?"

The earl's eyebrows arched upward in mild surprise. "My good child," he said, "did I not assure you, when I asked you to marry me, that I would make no such demands on you?"

"Oui, but —"

"And since that time, have I done anything to make you doubt that I am a man of my word?"

Lisette's face fell. *"Non,* milord." Setting down her cup, Lisette rose from the table.

"Will you not have a bit of toast? Buttered eggs, perhaps?"

"I have not anymore the hunger, milord," she said sadly, moving dejectedly toward the door.

"Lisette —"

She paused to turn back. *"Oui,* milord?"

"There is one thing that puzzles me. When you and I played piquet, you won almost every hand, and yet that damnable Frenchman was able to relieve you of your fan, your gloves, your shoes, and one of your stockings. I am at a loss to account for it."

He had all the felicity of seeing her melancholy vanish, and a mischievous smile light her expressive countenance. "Are you indeed, milord? But you knew that I cheated!"

On this Parthian shot, she nipped out of the room, leaving Waverly to address himself to the closed door. "Oh, Lisette," he murmured, chuckling, "what the devil am I going to do about you?"

He could think of only one possible solution. Abandoning his breakfast, he went to the library in search of pen and paper.

Helen, read the missive delivered by hand to Grosvenor Square some half-hour later, *I can wait no longer.* Lady Helen, to whose chamber this message was delivered along with her morning chocolate, sat bolt upright in her bed, her heart racing. Alas, a closer perusal of the letter revealed that the handwriting was not that of her husband. Nor, she reflected, frowning, would he be likely to express himself in terms better suited to Drury Lane than to private correspondence. Adjusting the pillows at her back, she continued to read. *Attend the Warburton ball tonight, and we will settle the matter once and for all. I will have a closed carriage waiting at eleven of the clock. I have given most of the servants the evening off, and will instruct the others not to wait up. We shall be quite alone. Yrs., etc., W.*

Lady Helen had hardly reached the end of this epistle when the connecting door opened to admit her husband.

"Good morning, Ethan," she said in a fair semblance of calm, reaching one hand out to him in greeting while, with the other, she deftly folded the missive and tucked it into the bodice of her dressing gown.

"Secrets, love?" he asked, observing this gesture as he took her proffered hand and raised it to his lips.

"Oh, the most tiresome thing! The Warburton ball is tonight. I promised to attend, but had forgotten all about it!"

"If you forgot it that easily, it can't be that important," pointed out Sir Ethan, perching on the edge of the bed and taking his wife in his arms. "Can't you get out of it?"

"Impossible!" declared Lady Helen, wriggling in his embrace in an effort to work Waverly's note deeper into the recesses of her bodice. "He — they will be expecting me."

"He, or they?"

"*They,* but most particularly *he,*" she said, pleased to be able to cover her slip without resorting to fabrication. "You see, Lord Warburton is an old friend of Papa's, and he is giving this ball to celebrate his wife's birthday. It would be very shabby of me to cry off."

Sir Ethan abandoned this forlorn hope with a shrug, then came to the purpose of his matutinal visit. " 'elen, I've been thinking," he said without preamble. "Let's go to Brighton."

They had gone to Brighton on their wedding trip. The memory was like salt in an open wound. "Brighton?" she echoed with a hollow laugh. "In the middle of the Season?"

"Why not?"

On the other hand, she reflected, Brighton was a very long way from Green Street. "I daresay Charles and William would enjoy sea-bathing —"

"The children are not invited," said Sir Ethan in a voice that brooked no argument. "They can stay in Town with their nurse, or if you'd rather, we can send them back to Lancashire."

"But, Ethan —"

"But me no buts! The last time we visited Brighton, we 'ad Sir Aubrey and Polly *and* the Dowager. This time it's going to be just you and me."

The note inside her bodice scratched her tender flesh, an all too painful reminder of how much had changed since their wedding trip to Brighton four years previously. Even if they left for Brighton tomorrow, it would never be the same. "I don't know, Ethan. I shall give it some thought."

With this he was forced to be content, so he kissed his wife's cheek and left her to the tender mercies of her dresser.

"What do you wish to wear today, my lady?" asked this personage somewhat dampeningly. Rose, it seemed, had no opinion of anyone who interrupted her mistress's toilette, husband or not.

"It doesn't matter — the lilac, I suppose."

"Very good, my lady," said the abigail, retrieving the lilac morning gown from the clothes-press. "And if you can tell me what you will want for the ball, I'll see that it's ready."

The question caught Lady Helen off guard. What did one wear for cuckolding one's husband? She joined Rose before the clothes-press and considered her options. White? No, virginal white seemed ludicrous, given the circumstances. Besides, she had worn white on that long-ago evening when she had first met her husband. The blue crape? No, for it was one of her favorites, and she wanted no ugly memories to spoil it for her. The jonquil satin with the lace overdress? Perfect! She had never liked it above half, and she was certain that after tonight she would loathe the very sight of it.

By the time Lady Helen returned to her room that evening to ready herself for the ball, the jonquil satin was neatly pressed and laid out on her bed. Alas, there was nothing at all neat or orderly about Lady Helen's thoughts. She looked forward to the evening with a perturbation of spirits unmatched since she had made her first curtsy eight years earlier. And to think that, upon that occasion, she had no greater fear than that of forgetting the steps of the cotillion or treading upon some gentleman's toes! How woefully naïve she must have been!

Her sensibilities notwithstanding, Lady Helen knew to a nicety how the game should be played. When the carriage set her down before the Warburtons' Belgrave

Square town house, she joined the receiving line with every appearance of pleasure. When she reached the top of the stairs and the butler announced her name, she greeted Lord Warburton warmly and wished Lady Warburton many happy returns of her natal day. When she entered the ballroom, she accepted a rather foppishly dressed viscount's offer to lead her into the set just forming. Not once did her gaze scan the crowded room for a glimpse of Lord Waverly, and no one watching her perform the complex patterns of the quadrille would have guessed just how much effort the omission required of her.

She had been at the ball for fully an hour before the familiar figure of the earl detached itself from the crowd and moved forward.

"Lady Helen," said Waverly, making his bow, "dare I hope the next dance is not yet taken?"

"Indeed, it is not, my lord," she replied, placing her gloved hand on his sleeve and allowing him to lead her back onto the floor. The next set was a contredanse, whose movements repeatedly paired couples only to tear them apart, so their conversation was brief, and marked by fits and starts.

"I have not seen your husband this evening," Waverly observed. "Does he not accompany you?"

"Ethan dined at his club tonight. I daresay he is still there."

"How very accommodating of him, to be sure."

As the movement of the dance required that the earl surrender her temporarily to a portly baron, Lady Helen offered no comment to this remark, but when the steps reunited them, asked a question of her own.

"And Lisette?"

"She has gone to the theatre with a party of young people, and will not return until well after midnight." He lowered his voice. "So as you see, we need not fear interruption."

Once again the steps of the dance separated them, so Lady Helen merely nodded in acknowledgement. Everything was proceeding according to plan, and by morning, revenge would be hers. She should be pleased. Why, then, did she keep glancing at the long-case clock along the wall, wishing she might slow the hands that moved inexorably toward eleven?

❦

In his assessment of his wife's whereabouts, Lord Waverly was only partially

203

correct. To be sure, Lisette had indeed attended a performance of *Laugh When You Can* at Drury Lane with a party of young people; however, as the curtain fell on the first act, the group dispersed in search of food, friends, and flirtations. Lisette elected to remain alone in the box, and it was here that Étienne found her.

"*Bon soir,* Madame Waverly," he said, advancing tentatively into the box.

Lisette turned and, recognizing the speaker, promptly turned her back on him. "*Bon soir, monsieur,*" she said frostily.

"Forgive me, madame," the Frenchman continued in some agitation. "I know your husband commanded me to keep my distance, but under the circumstances, I feel sure he would understand — even approve of — my approaching you."

Lisette again turned to face him. "*Oui?* I wonder, *monsieur,* what makes you think so?"

"I do not wish to distress you, but there has been an accident — your husband —"

Lisette's icy demeanor melted in an instant. "Milord? Is he badly hurt?"

"Not being a doctor, I would not presume to judge —"

"You must take me to him at once!" Lisette demanded, leaping to her feet.

"*Très bien,* if that is what you wish —"

Lisette stamped her foot impatiently. "At once! *Comprenez-vous?*"

She did not wait for a reply, but flung herself through the curtain in a swirl of pink satin.

"As you wish," Étienne said meekly to the empty air, then followed her from the box.

By the time he caught up with her, she had reached the street, where she hailed a hackney in a torrent of impassioned French.

"Where to, miss?" asked the driver of this equipage, drawing up beside her.

Lisette, finding herself at a loss, turned to Étienne. "Where is he?"

"It is my understanding that he was taken to a hostel in Southwark. Great Dover Street," he added for the driver's benefit, as he handed Lisette into the carriage.

"*Mais non!*" Lisette protested, one foot poised on the step. "We must go at once to Park Lane and have everything made ready for his return. I will not allow milord to die in a hovel!"

"Not a hovel; a hostel," Étienne corrected her.

But Lisette would not be swayed. "I am

sure they are very much the same thing. To Park Lane — *vite!*" she commanded the driver.

This individual had no knowledge of French, but everything in his passenger's manner bespoke her need for haste. Besides which, he had always had a soft spot for a pretty young thing, even if she was a foreigner. He whipped up the horses just as Étienne entered the carriage behind Lisette, and the equipage barreled westward toward Park Lane.

Étienne, finding himself tumbled unceremoniously onto the floor of the carriage, scrambled to his feet with what dignity he could muster, pulled the door shut, and collapsed onto the seat. Within a very few minutes, the carriage rolled to a stop before Lord Waverly's town house. Lisette flung open the door and, not waiting for the step to be let down, leaped to the ground. With Étienne hurrying to keep up, she scampered up the stairs to the portico and burst into the foyer.

"There has been an accident," she informed the startled butler. "Milord is injured. I will bring him home very shortly. Send a footman for *le médecin*, and have Cook boil water and prepare a broth. Tell milord's *valet de chambre* to make up a bed on the ground floor, and to find bandages. He may tear up the sheets in the blue bed-chamber, if necessary."

The butler, astounded at the sight of his youthful mistress taking command like the countess she was, could only stare open-mouthed.

"*Tout de suite*," commanded Lisette impatiently, stamping her foot. "At once, do you hear?"

"Yes, madam," he said hastily. "Right away, madam."

"And now," she pronounced, turning back to Étienne, "you will take me to this hovel in Great Dover Street where is milord."

Étienne, recognizing his cue, took Lisette's arm and ushered her back outside to the hackney carriage, whose driver waited impatiently for his fare.

"That'll be a shilling and sixpence, that will," he informed Étienne in a manner calculated to inform him that he did not intend to be taken advantage of by a foreigner.

"But we have not yet done with your services," Étienne protested. "Take us at once to the Pig and Whistle, in Great Dover Street."

"I'll not be taking you nowhere until I

get my shilling and six," reiterated the driver, thrusting his cupped hand belligerently at the Frenchman.

"Oh, very well," muttered Étienne, shoving his hand into the pocket of his breeches. Having paid the driver, he climbed into the carriage and seated himself beside Lisette. As the vehicle lurched forward, he patted her hand consolingly. "There, now! You'll be with your husband again very soon."

Lisette, however, had by this time recalled her grudge against him, and removed herself to the rear-facing seat. "I will accept your escort to Great Dover Street because I must, but until we arrive there, you will please be so good as not to touch me again."

"Lisette — Madame Waverly — you have every reason to be angry with me," Étienne said coaxingly. "You see, I thought your husband could have no objections to your entertaining another gentleman's attentions. I supposed your marriage to Lord Waverly must be a *mariage de covenance,* a — how shall I say it? A purely financial arrangement."

"A financial arrangement?" echoed Lisette, her brow wrinkling in a puzzled frown. "In what way?"

"Milord Waverly left England under a cloud of scandal and bankruptcy, and has lived in Paris for the last several years with gaming as his only source of income. When I learned that he had wed you and taken you back to England, I imagined — pardon my bluntness! — that he must have married you for your money."

"*What* money, *s'il vous plaît?*"

"Why, your inheritance from your English *grand-père*," explained Étienne. "But when milord Waverly was so very angry at our, er, indiscretion, I saw at once that I was mistaken."

"But I have no inheritance!" Bright spots of color burned in Lisette's cheeks. "It is too absurd!"

"Of course you do not," Étienne assured her. "I merely supposed that you, being his only grandchild, must have inherited his considerable fortune."

Had she the leisure to examine this statement, Lisette might have wondered at the source of Étienne's considerable information. But having undergone a series of revelations in less than half an hour, from the news that her husband might be on his deathbed, to the possibility that she might be the possessor of a considerable fortune, and the subsequent suggestion that her injured husband might have married her for the sake of said fortune, Lisette was in no fit state to consider Étienne's argument rationally.

"It does not matter whether I have the inheritance or not!" she declared passionately, as much to herself as to her travelling companion. "Milord married me because he is good, and honorable, and would not abandon me in a foreign land!"

"I am sure you are right," said Étienne reassuringly. "After all, who would know Milord Waverly better than his own wife? I am certain it is just as you say, and anything between him and the Lady Hélène Brundy is all in the past."

Lisette drew breath to hotly deny any connection, past or present, between her husband and Lady Helen, but the words stuck in her throat, refusing to be uttered. She no longer trusted Étienne, for anyone who would lure her to such indiscretion as he had at the Dorrington ball was assuredly no true friend. She could not believe a word he said. And yet, there were things, small things, to be sure, but things which, when taken together, made her fear that in this instance, at least, Étienne might be telling her the truth.

"Ah, here it is, the Pig and Whistle!" declared Étienne cheerfully, apparently oblivious to Lisette's inner struggle. "We have arrived!"

Surely when she saw him again, all these terrible doubts would be put to rest. He would laugh at her and call her a foolish child, and they would be happy again. Unless, the dreadful thought occurred to her, he was so badly injured that he could not speak. Perhaps he might even die, and she would never know the truth. Without waiting for Étienne, she wrenched open the door and leaped from the carriage before the wheels had stopped rolling, and ran into the hostel where her husband waited.

"Welcome to the Pig and Whistle, miss," said the proprietor of this establishment, bowing to his elegantly clad visitor. "How can I helps you this evenin'?"

"A man was brought here earlier, a gentleman who was injured," Lisette explained hurriedly. "Where is he now?"

"There's a gentleman in the private parlor to your right, miss, but he's not —"

"*Merci,*" said Lisette, not lingering to hear more. Turning to the closed door on her right, she tried the knob and, finding it unlocked, hurried inside.

She froze on the threshold. She had expected to find her husband lying on a make-shift bed, or perhaps the sofa, wrapped in blood-soaked bandages and groaning in pain. Instead, a fire burned merrily in the grate, and a wing chair had been drawn up before the blaze to take advantage of its warmth. The chair's high back blocked Lisette's view of the man seated there, but that there was a man she had no doubt: his booted foot stretched out toward the hearth, the flames casting dancing reflections off the glossy black leather.

"Milord?" Lisette asked, advancing tentatively into the room.

"*Non, je regrette.*" The gentleman rose to meet her, revealing a pair of close-set black eyes over a long nose and pointy chin. "But perhaps you will have a word of welcome for your Cousin Raoul?"

"Raoul!" Lisette fairly spat the word. "What have you done with milord Waverly?"

Raoul spread his hands in a gesture indicative of innocence. "Why, nothing, *ma cousine!* I have seen him only once, and that was many weeks ago in Amiens."

"But he was here! Étienne said —" Lisette's eyes grew round as, too late, she realized the full extent of her countryman's perfidy. She spun toward the door, and found Étienne leaning negligently against the doorframe. "I will have the truth now, *s'il vous plaît.* Milord was not here, was he? In fact, he was never injured at all."

Étienne bowed. "You will be pleased to know milord Waverly enjoys his customary good health."

"Then why — ?"

"I have come to take you home," said Raoul. "I am to be married, and your presence is required."

"Married? To whom?"

"Why, to you, *cherie.*"

"I am sorry to disappoint you, Raoul, but I am already wed."

"Faugh!" scoffed Raoul. "Do you truly think that such a marriage — contracted by a minor to an Englishman in a Protestant ceremony — would be recognized by the Church, let alone the courts?"

In truth, Lisette did not know what to think or whom to believe. She had no doubt that her cousin would not hesitate to further his cause with lies; indeed, had she entertained any doubts on this head, Étienne's betrayal would have by this time put them to rest. And one of his claims, at least, she now knew to be true. She was now quite certain that she must be a great heiress, as Étienne had claimed, for she could think of no other reason why Raoul would scheme to marry a cousin for whom he had never felt any emotion more tender than mild annoyance. And if this claim were true, then perhaps his other arguments were equally true. If his insinuations regarding her marriage to Lord Waverly were correct, it would explain why the earl was in no hurry to consummate the union. There was even the possibility that Waverly had not insisted upon a second, Catholic, ceremony in order to give himself an escape route, should Lady Helen suddenly become free. The greater the number of possibilities which presented themselves to her, the more confused she became. She wanted nothing more than to clap her hands over her ears, blotting out the whispered innuendoes that overwhelmed her, but she knew this would accomplish nothing: the voices that now mocked her were inside her own head.

As if aware of Lisette's inner turmoil (and his own imminent victory), Raoul regarded her with a smug smile. "Admit it, *ma cousine*, what choice do you have? You have run away from your convent and cohabited with a man to whom you may or may not be legally wed. You are a disgrace to your vocation, Lisette, as well as to your family. Fortunately, for the sake of our family's honor —"

"Much you know about honor!" retorted Lisette.

Raoul's face darkened. "For the sake of our family's honor," he repeated slowly, "I am willing to give you the protection of my name."

"If that is protection, I think I would do better to manage on my own," said Lisette, adding in a voice of exaggerated politeness, "Thank you, cousin, but I must decline your generous offer."

Raoul bared his teeth in a feral smile. "I wonder, *ma cousine,* what makes you think you have any choice in the matter?"

He took a step forward, and Lisette, seeing him advancing upon her, whirled around and made for the door. But Étienne was there, flinging out his arm to block the way. She grabbed at his arm, clawing at him, but to no avail. Raoul seized her from behind, and though she fought and scratched at him, the end was never in doubt. Finally, seizing her by the hair, he pinned her against his chest while Étienne covered her nose and mouth with a noxious-smelling handkerchief. Lisette's body went limp, all her questions temporarily silenced.

12

It is the wished, the trysted hour.
ROBERT BURNS, *Mary Morison*

While Lisette confronted her cousin, Lady
Helen, seated beside Lord Waverly in his
carriage, moved inexorably toward a confrontation of quite another kind. They had
departed the Warburton ball promptly at
eleven, as planned. Now every revolution of
the carriage's wheels brought them closer to
Park Lane and, ultimately, her revenge upon
a faithless spouse. No, she told herself resolutely, she would not think of Ethan now.
She would concentrate on the task at hand.
She was, after all, the daughter of a duke; she
had been taught all her life that one of the
obligations of high position was the necessity
of performing certain duties, no matter how
unpleasant — nay, even repellent! — one
might find them. Being female, she had been
given to understand that foremost among
these necessary evils was the conjugal bed;

how ironic that in her case, the dreaded task was not the consummation of a legal union, but the formation of an illicit one!

All too soon, the carriage slowed and rolled to a stop before Lord Waverly's town house. The earl (who, like his inamorata, had been unusually silent throughout the drive) stepped down and offered his arm. Lady Helen placed her gloved hand upon it, and allowed him to escort her up the shallow steps to the front door now looming before her. By the time she passed through it again, she would have betrayed the husband she loved more than life, in the most elemental way a woman could betray a man. As Lord Waverly reached for the knob, something inside her snapped.

"No, I cannot!" she cried, pulling her hand away. "I am sorry, Waverly — I thought I could — but I cannot!"

What Lord Waverly might have said to this outburst would never be known, for at that moment the door was flung open, revealing a host of worried-looking servants in a hall ablaze with light.

"Your lordship!" exclaimed Reynolds, his usually impassive demeanor slipping. "Thank God!"

"If I may say so, it is a relief to know that her ladyship's fears were exaggerated," observed Waverly's valet, mincing forward to relieve the earl of his cloak, gloves, and chapeau bras. "Still, should you not feel up to climbing the stairs, you will find a makeshift bed prepared for you in the drawing room."

"Indeed, my lord, you won't wish to overtax your strength," blustered a stout stranger bearing a bulging leather bag. "If your lordship will repair to the drawing room, I will examine the wound."

Lord Waverly, who had listened with some bewilderment to the chorus which greeted his arrival, now spoke. "Who the devil are *you?*"

"Sir Robert Franklin, physician," replied this worthy, offering his card. "I was given to understand that your lordship's case was urgent. Permit me to say that I am relieved to discover this is apparently not the case."

"I will permit you," said Lord Waverly with great deliberation, "to tell me what in God's name you're doing in my house!"

"It was Lady Waverly, my lord," offered Reynolds. "She returned early from the theatre, convinced that your lordship had met with an accident. She was most distraught, if I may say so."

"Was she?" asked Waverly, a bemused smile playing about his mouth. "I wonder what can have given her such an idea?"

"I do not know, sir. I was under the impression that the gentleman who accompanied my lady must have brought her the erroneous report."

The smile was wiped from Waverly's lips. "Gentleman? What gentleman?"

"Why, the Frenchman who called upon my lady only last week. I know your instructions were to deny him the house, my lord, but under the circumstances —"

"Yes, yes, never mind that! Where are they now?"

"They departed almost at once, my lord, her ladyship having formed the intention of, er, flying to your lordship's side to offer succor."

"Damn! They must have arrived at the Warburtons' house by now!"

"Begging your pardon, my lord, but they were not bound for the Warburton ball. The gentleman informed my lady that you were in Southwark."

"Southwark? What the deuce would I be doing in Southwark?"

"I do not know, sir. I only heard him tell my lady that you might be found at a hostel in Great Dover Street."

"Great Dover — Good God!" Grabbing Lady Helen by the arm, he propelled her toward the door, lingering only long enough to toss over his shoulder to Reynolds, "I am going after Lady Waverly. With any luck, I shall return shortly; otherwise, I shall send word as soon as I am able."

Back in the street, Waverly bundled Lady Helen into the carriage, barked a curt order to the driver, and ducked inside, closing the door behind him as the vehicle surged forward.

"What is the matter?" asked Lady Helen as they turned into Piccadilly, her interrupted rendezvous all but forgotten. "Why do you suppose they have gone to Southwark?"

He blinked at her, as if surprised to find her still there. "I do not think they have gone to Southwark at all."

"Then where are we going?"

"My dear Helen, if one takes Great Dover Street and drives straight on, without stopping, where will one eventually find oneself?"

"In Dover, I suppose," she said with a shrug.

He nodded. "Then that is where we are going."

"To *Dover?*" she gasped. "I cannot possibly accompany you all the way to Dover!"

"On the contrary. If we reach Dover and find they have already sailed for France, you will accompany me a great deal farther than that."

"You cannot be serious!" But one look at Waverly's resolute profile was enough to convince her that he was in deadly earnest. "No! I will not go with you! Take me home at once!"

"I am sorry. That is quite impossible."

"But — but I have a husband and children who will be expecting me! What will Ethan think?"

"He will no doubt think exactly what you have wanted him to think for the past fortnight," replied the earl with brutal candor.

"But I *don't* want him to!" Lady Helen insisted. "I still love him, and I could never betray him, no matter what he has done!"

"Your sentiments are vastly touching, my dear, but to be perfectly honest, I find your marital difficulties are rapidly becoming a bit of a bore."

Lady Helen opened her mouth to protest, then changed her mind. "I — see," she said at last, regarding Lord Waverly as if seeing him with new eyes. "Tell me, Waverly — how long have you been in love with Lisette?"

"In love?" Waverly bristled, but the wildly swaying carriage lamp revealed his suddenly heightened color. "Balderdash!"

"No, I do not think so — in fact, I am certain of it," declared Lady Helen, warming to this theme. "Since the day of my marriage — even before, one might argue — you have expressed your desire for, er, an intimate connection with me. And yet, when such a connection was at last within your reach, you delayed in seizing your opportunity, choosing again and again to go to Lisette instead. Indeed, I am amazed I did not see it before."

"If I neglected you for Lisette, it was because I trusted you to behave with discretion. I could place no such dependence upon Lisette; in fact, I have had to guard her like a duenna to keep her from ruining my good name!"

Far from being persuaded by this argument, Lady Helen choked back a peal of laughter. "No, Waverly, how can you say so? When your good name has been in ruins any time these four years!"

"*Touché*," he acknowledged with a wry twist of his mouth. "Now tell me, does it seem likely to you that such a ramshackle fellow as I should succumb to the charms of a seventeen-year-old?"

"No," Lady Helen confessed. "In fact, I should think she would be the last sort of girl to appeal to you. Still, it seems to me that if you did *not* love her, you would be very grateful to have her taken off your hands, rather than practically kidnapping me and haring across the countryside in pursuit."

"Kidnapping you, Helen? Nonsense! You came with me quite willingly; in fact, as I recall, the whole thing was done at your instigation."

"Oh, do let us argue semantics, Waverly!" Lady Helen applauded. "They serve so well to distract one's attention from the subject at hand!"

Lord Waverly muttered something to the effect that Lady Helen's weaver might have her with his blessing, and turned to stare moodily out the window.

🍎

Had they but known it, Lord Waverly and Lady Helen were by this time not only the pursuers, but the pursued. For Sir Ethan Brundy, finding none of his particular cronies in attendance at Brooks's that evening, had ample opportunity to consider the state of his marriage as he partook of his solitary supper. It was not a pleasant exercise, but he had every hope that it might prove to be a profitable one. As he recalled his parting with his wife, he realized that although he had tried to persuade her to change her plans to accommodate him, he had made no effort to do the same for her. Had he, over the past four years, made a practice of such self-serving behavior? He did not think so, but then, there were times, particularly of late, when dealing with his wife had left him with the lowering suspicion that he was really quite amazingly stupid. In any case, attending one rather tedious ball was surely not so great a sacrifice, especially when the future of one's marriage might well be at stake.

His mind made up, he had collected his hat and gloves from the porter and set out on foot for Warburton House. He had reached it just as the church bells tolled eleven o'clock. The evening's festivities were apparently still in full swing; only one solitary vehicle, a dark crested coach, waited in front to convey its owner home. The house was ablaze with lights, and violin music wafted outward on the night breeze — louder now, as the front door opened to permit the exit of a fair-haired lady in a light-colored gown. Sir Ethan's heart swelled as he recognized the identity of the lady seemingly coming to meet him, but even as he moved forward to greet her, the silhouetted figure of a man emerged from the waiting carriage and handed her inside. Sir Ethan could only stare in bewilderment as the door closed behind the pair and the carriage began to move forward. As it drew abreast of one of the newly installed gas lamps, the streetlight illuminated the coat of arms emblazoned on the door: the crest of the earl of Waverly.

The discovery jolted Sir Ethan into action. He ran after the carriage for some dozen steps before, recognizing the futility of this exercise, he gave up the attempt and turned his attention instead to summoning a hackney.

"You, there!" he shouted to a promising, if unprepossessing, vehicle trolling the area in search of departing revelers desirous of transportation.

"Where to, guv'nor?" asked the driver, drawing to a halt.

Sir Ethan did not trouble to open the door, but instead clambered up onto the box beside the driver. "Follow that carriage!"

Unfortunately, the earl had by now a considerable head start, besides the not inconsiderable advantage of knowing where he was going. Sir Ethan soon lost sight of his quarry, though not before seeing enough of the route to form a very good idea of the final destination.

"Park Lane," he predicted to his companion on the box. "That's where 'e'll be 'eaded. Take me to Park Lane. Number eleven."

When they reached Lord Waverly's town house, however, there was no sign of the carriage. Either he had been wrong in his estimation, or the carriage had already delivered its passengers and returned to the mews. One way or the other, Sir Ethan was determined to find out. He leaped down from the box, marched up the steps, and pounded on the door. It was opened almost at once by a butler curiously unsurprised by the lateness of the visit.

"All right, where is she?" Sir Ethan demanded, striding past this unflappable individual.

The butler cleared his throat deprecatingly. "Naturally, I am not in my lady's confidence, sir, but I understand that she has gone to an inn in Southwark."

Whatever Sir Ethan had expected — and his imagination had provided many possible scenarios during the short drive — it was not that. "An inn in — and 'is lordship too, I suppose?"

Reynolds inclined his head in the affirmative.

"And did she seem —" He hardly knew how to ask the question. "— Unwilling? Did she struggle?"

Reynolds was eager to reassure the caller on this point. "Oh no, sir, not at all. She was a bit distraught — which, if I may say so, was not to be wondered at, under the circumstances — but she was determined that his lordship's bed should be properly warmed."

This bald confirmation of his worst fears made Sir Ethan feel ill. The obliging Reynolds, noting his ashen color, felt it incumbent upon him to offer the visitor refreshment until such time as he might see for himself that Lord Waverly's injuries had been greatly exaggerated.

"If you will have a glass of brandy in the green saloon, sir, they should return very shortly."

Sir Ethan had never needed a brandy more, but every feeling revolted at the suggestion that he should sit meekly by while his old adversary planted cuckold's horns on his head.

"No brandy, I'll — Southwark, you said?"

"Yes, sir. The Pig and Whistle, in Great Dover Street."

Armed with this information, Sir Ethan saw no reason to linger. He bounded down the steps to the street, where the driver of the hackney walked his horses while waiting impatiently for his fare.

"Take me to the Pig and Whistle in Great Dover Street," Sir Ethan commanded.

"That's on t'other side of the river," the driver observed.

"Aye, so we'd best get a move on."

"I don't go beyond Blackfriars Bridge."

"I'll make it worth your while," promised Sir Ethan.

"I don't go beyond Blackfriars Bridge," reiterated the driver, not without satisfaction.

Sir Ethan reached for the leather purse in the pocket of his coat. " 'ow much for the coach and pair?"

The man goggled. "Beg pardon, guv'nor?"

"I'm going to Southwark, and I'm going in your carriage," declared Sir Ethan in a voice that brooked no argument. "You can either be paid for it, or you can summon the watch and tell 'im it's been stolen."

A moment's reflection on the competence of the local law enforcement was sufficient to inform the driver as to the wisest

228

course. Sir Ethan, correctly interpreting the man's unspoken assent, pressed into his hand a roll of bank notes far in excess of the antiquated vehicle's worth, then climbed onto the box, whipped up the horses, and disappeared into the night.

13

Between the devil and the deep blue sea.
ANONYMOUS

Lisette awoke to find herself on a narrow cot that lurched beneath her. A small gray circle of light set into the wall over her head hinted at the approach of dawn. Clearly, several hours had elapsed since her confrontation with her cousin Raoul. But what had happened during that time? Where was Raoul now? More importantly, where was *she?*

Groggily, Lisette scrambled to her knees to peer out the little round window. The cot lurched again, and Lisette realized that its motion was not merely an aftereffect of the noxious stuff Raoul had held over her nose: beyond the porthole, whitecaps tossed in the wind. This could not be the Thames, she reasoned, for there was no land in sight. And yet, even without landmarks, there was something familiar — of course! She had traversed this particular body of water once before, under happier circumstances. The French called it *la Manche*, the sleeve; the English, with the unthinking arrogance characteristic of their breed, referred to it as the English Channel. She was being taken back to France and, presumably, to a forced marriage with her cousin Raoul. She must escape! But how? Even had the porthole been large enough for her to squeeze through, she could hardly leap overboard and swim to shore. On the other hand, drowning in the attempt would be preferable to life as Raoul's wife.

As Lisette wrestled with indecision, a rattling at the door took the matter out of her hands. She collapsed back onto the cot and shut her eyes just as the door creaked open.

"See?" came the contemptible voice of her cousin. "It is as I have said. She is still asleep. If fortune smiles upon us, she will remain so until we reach Calais."

"And then?" asked Étienne. "You must know that her husband will come for her. He is insanely jealous, that one."

"Ah, but you do not understand the English. Was not my own English uncle, Lisette's *père*, disinherited by his own father for making a *mésalliance?* And in his case, there was no title to be considered. Believe me, milord will relinquish all claim to Lisette when he learns that she may bear him a bastard heir."

Étienne bristled. "I may have persuaded her to an indiscreet game of cards, but as God is my witness, I never —"

"No, for you had not the sense to!" retorted Raoul. "As it happens, I was not speaking of you, but of myself. By the time her husband arrives, I will have arranged for a priest to join us in marriage — and you may be sure I will lose no time in consummating the union. Between the scandal of a bigamous bride and the threat to his lineage, the English earl will be only too thankful to wash his hands of her."

A gasp escaped Lisette's lips in spite of her best efforts, and both men whirled to confront her.

"Aha! So Étienne was right, and you are awake."

Since to deny it would be an exercise in futility, Lisette allowed her eyes to flutter open. "*Oui,* I am awake, but I feel most unwell. It is just as it was when milord brought me from France."

Raoul regarded his cousin with an arrested expression. "You suffered from the *mal de mer?*"

"*Oui,* so much so that I wished I were dead," Lisette lied without hesitation. "Even after we landed at Dover, it was many days before I was sufficiently recovered to go on."

Raoul looked somewhat daunted at this unexpected obstacle to his plans. "Well," he blustered, "perhaps the wind will die down and you will feel better directly."

"Perhaps. Until then, if you please, I should like to lie quietly and rest. I would prefer to be alone."

Suspicion crossed Raoul's face. "I do not trust you, *ma cousine.* I had rather stay with you."

Lisette turned away with a weak shrug. "As you wish. Perhaps you would be so kind as to bring for me a basin? I am feeling — most — unwell —"

Clapping both hands forebodingly over her mouth, Lisette managed to hide her satisfied smile as Raoul took to his heels.

❦

However much Lisette might relish this minor triumph over her wicked cousin, she had more trials to endure before her victory was complete. Knowing that escape was impossible until they had landed at Calais, she feigned illness for the rest of the journey, lying on her cot and moaning pathetically every time the door opened to admit her jailers bringing food or drink. As the hours passed, this ruse became increasingly difficult to maintain, for the bowl of chicken broth Étienne pressed upon her emitted a most tempting aroma, and Lisette, having left the theatre before her party returned to the box with refreshments, was by this time quite hungry. Still, she knew what she must do, so she regarded the bowl with a tortured look which might have been revulsion or longing, and resolutely turned her face away.

At length they docked at Calais. Lisette closed her eyes and feigned semi-consciousness as Raoul entered her cabin without knocking and hoisted her up into his arms. Although his hot breath on her cheek and his ungentle hands on her body made her make-believe illness seem all too real, Lisette forced herself to remain limp in his hold as he carried her first up to the deck, then down the gangplank. If she did not struggle in his hold, neither did she make any attempt to lighten his load. As a result, she was pleased to note, Raoul's breathing had become somewhat labored by the time he located a dark little waterfront inn.

"Innkeeper!" he called as he entered this establishment with Lisette in his arms and

Étienne at his heels. "A room, *s'il vous plaît,* for myself and my wife."

"And another for me," put in Étienne.

No one paid him the slightest heed. The innkeeper looked askance at the drooping, disheveled woman in evening dress. Raoul, seeing that some explanation was called for, fairly oozed oily charm.

"She is most unwell, as you can see. The *mal de mer,* you know." He heaved an indulgent sigh. "Ah well, we cannot all be robust travelers, and she always was a delicate creature. I am certain a night's rest at this fine establishment will soon have her on her feet again."

The innkeeper nodded slowly, apparently accepting this explanation at face value. "This way, *messieurs, madame.*"

The staircase was too narrow to allow for their walking abreast, so the innkeeper stepped back to allow his guests to go first. "The first door on the right, just past —"

He broke off abruptly, for the young woman was now not only fully conscious, but casting pleading eyes at him and mouthing, in French, *"Help me! I am being kidnapped! Help me escape!"*

His gallant instincts fully roused, he halted just before they reached the top of the stairs. "On second thought, *madame*

235

might rest more comfortably in the last room on the left. It overlooks the kitchen garden, so she will be undisturbed by the noise from the street."

Raoul thanked the man and, after entering the back chamber the innkeeper had suggested, deposited Lisette with every appearance of tenderness onto the bed. Although the innkeeper and Étienne left the room, Raoul did not follow right away, and for one horrific moment Lisette feared he intended to remain. Fortunately, he lingered only long enough to ensure that his host did not witness the spectacle of the concerned husband locking his ailing wife in her room. Having accomplished this task, Raoul went back down the stairs in search of his crony.

Lisette, finding herself mercifully alone, waited only until the sound of his footsteps had been swallowed up by the clamor in the taproom below. She bounded off the bed, crossed to the single window, and drew back the curtains. As the innkeeper had said, the window looked down upon the kitchen garden. What he had *not* said was that it also looked directly into the crown of an ancient apple tree, one of whose boughs stretched invitingly toward the window.

Lisette did not hesitate. She pulled off her flimsy evening slippers and stuffed them into her *décolletage,* pushed open the casement, and hoisted herself through the window and into the welcoming arms of the tree.

To one who had recently scaled the wall at Sainte-Marie, scurrying down a generously forked tree posed no very great difficulty, although the enterprise left Lisette's once-elegant opera gown very much the worse for wear, and her stockings little more than a tangle of silk threads. All in all, however, she considered it a small price to pay for freedom. Upon reaching *terra firma,* she withdrew her slippers from her bodice and stepped into them, then stole furtively into the narrow lane at the back of the inn.

Her freedom thus won, Lisette had no very clear idea of where to go. She had no acquaintance in Calais; indeed, she had set foot in the town only once before in her life, and that only long enough for Lord Waverly to book passage to England. Her impressions of the place were vague, but she remembered the waterfront, the old town hall with its thirteenth-century clock tower, the lace factories, the convent of Sainte-Jeanne —

Lisette's steps slowed to a halt. Did she dare seek refuge at a convent? Would the story of her escape from Sainte-Marie have spread this far? As she hesitated, the door of a nearby tavern flew open, and three fishermen staggered out. At the sight of an attractive and appealingly disheveled young woman, they leered appreciatively, one going so far as to weave his way unsteadily across the road in her direction. Lisette, surmising at a glance that all inebriates were not so gentlemanly as Lord Waverly, debated no longer, but took to her heels.

At length she reached the stone wall with its heavy iron gate which connected the residents of Sainte-Jeanne to — and isolated them from — the outside world. She tugged on the bell rope, and a moment later a nun in black habit and wimple answered her summons.

"*S'il vous plaît,*" Lisette began, "I have been abducted, and only just escaped from my captors. I have come to beg asylum."

Even as she spoke the words, Lisette wondered if anyone could truly believe such a fantastic story. She did not realize that her bedraggled curls and torn and dirty gown — to say nothing of the fearful glance she cast over her shoulder — did more than any words to convince the wary sister of her very real distress.

"*Un instant*," came the reply. "I will ask *Mamère*."

After what seemed to Lisette an eternity (but was in reality less than five minutes) the nun returned with a large iron key. "*Mamère* will see you," she said, turning the key in the lock and swinging the gate open. "If you will please to follow me?"

The sound of the gate clanging shut behind her filled Lisette with a sense of foreboding, and as they crossed the cloister and entered the Mother Superior's chamber, her heart began to pound against her ribs.

"Come in," called a woman's voice from inside the chamber.

Lisette entered, and felt almost dizzy with relief at the sight of the compassionate woman smiling serenely at her.

"*Ma pauvre enfant*," said the Mother Superior, holding out her hands. "It appears you have had a difficult time. Sister Margaret will see that you have something to eat, a bath, and a change of clothes. I hope you will not object to a novice's habit? I fear it is all we have to offer."

Lisette fell to her knees before the kindly woman and kissed her hand. "*Non,*

Mamère, not at all. But before I accept your kindness, I must tell you that I was once a novice at the convent of Sainte-Marie in Paris. I — I ran away."

However much this confession might have shocked the Mother Superior, it said much to her credit that she showed no sign of disapproval, nor was there any cooling in her manner toward the penitent. "Perhaps it will make you feel better to tell me how this came about, *oui?*"

Thus encouraged, Lisette took a deep breath. She told the whole story, beginning with her aunt and uncle's hopes for her marriage to her cousin, and continuing on through her escape from the convent with Lord Waverly's assistance, their journey to England and subsequent marriage. Had she but known it, the glow in her eyes when she first brought Lord Waverly onto her stage told the wise nun by inference a great deal that Lisette never put into words.

"And now," Lisette concluded miserably, "Étienne tells me that I am a great heiress, and that milord only wished to marry me for my fortune, which I did not even know that I had, and — oh, *Mamère,* I very much fear that he may be right! Tell me, do you think it is a — a judgment upon me for running away from Sainte-Marie?"

The Mother Superior deliberated for a long moment before making her pronouncement. "I cannot speak for the Almighty but, while I do know He works in mysterious ways, I cannot imagine how even He might expect to encourage virtue by rewarding vice with a handsome and gallant husband! *Non*, child, it appears to me that the sin in this case belongs to your aunt and uncle, in forcing you to choose between a husband you could not respect and a vocation to which you were not called." She raised Lisette to her feet by the hand still clasping hers. "But I must remind you that it is not for me to decide. The chapel is open; had you not best discuss the matter with *le bon Dieu* Himself?"

❦

"*Alors*," pronounced Raoul over a bottle of his host's excellent sherry, "all is settled. Father Claude will be here within the hour to perform the ceremony."

"*Oui*, so it appears," Étienne agreed doubtfully. "Still, I wish I might know where milord Waverly is at this moment."

Étienne's wish was about to be realized, for at that moment a commotion at the door heralded the arrival of the next packet from Dover. The travelers surged into the inn to procure refreshments, lodging, or transportation to points further inland. As the throng vied for the inn-keeper's attention, one man stood apart from the crowd, his attention fixed instead on a survey of the taproom. He was tall, dark, and strangely compelling even though his rumpled evening clothes should have appeared ridiculously out of place. Étienne, recognizing him, would have turned his face away, had he not been momentarily distracted by the earl's companion, a stunningly beautiful woman also clad in evening attire. Here Étienne's appreciation of feminine beauty betrayed him, for while he assayed Lady Helen's charms, Lord Waverly caught sight of Lisette's erstwhile admirer and headed straight for him.

Upon reaching the table, however, it was not Étienne to whom the earl addressed himself, but Raoul. His communication was brief and to the point.

"All right, where is she?"

"I don't know what you are talking about," Raoul said, looking him squarely in the eye.

Lord Waverly bared his teeth in a smile with little warmth and less humor. "I think you do."

"That, sir, is your misfortune."

Waverly seized the weasel-faced Frenchman by the cravat and hauled him to his feet. "By God, if you have harmed one hair on her head —"

"I tell you, I don't know what you mean!" declared Raoul, white-faced but unwavering. "Perhaps you have mistaken me for someone else."

"I don't think so. Innkeeper!" Waverly called to the hôtelier, and somehow his voice penetrated the crowd demanding service. "It seems these two gentlemen have forgotten their room assignments. Can you perhaps oblige them?"

"*Oui, monsieur*," replied this worthy. "Upstairs and down the corridor. Last two doors on the left."

"*Merci.*"

Waverly released his hold on Raoul's neckcloth, and the Frenchman collapsed back into his chair. Taking Lady Helen by the arm, the earl led her in the direction of the staircase.

"Wait!" cried Étienne, throwing out an arm to forestall them. "As you have surmised, we have escorted Lisette — Lady Waverly, that is — back to France. Her aunt and uncle, you must know, miss her dreadfully. And since she was reluctant to leave you, my lord, we were obliged to take certain measures to, er, persuade her, but I swear to you there is nothing the matter with her save a case of the *mal de mer!*"

To his astonishment, Lord Waverly laughed. "The *mal de mer?* I fear my wife has been making a May game of you, M. Villiers. Lisette was never seasick a day in her life."

"I assure you, my lord, she —"

"*What?*" demanded Raoul. "*Not* sick, you say? Why, I'll —"

Livid with rage, he shot up from the table and took the stairs two at a stride. Étienne, Lord Waverly, and Lady Helen hurried after him. They caught up with him just as he turned the key in the lock and flung the door open. The bed, though rumpled, was unoccupied. The curtains swayed gently in the breeze from an open window. Raoul strode across the room to it, tore the curtains back, and found himself staring into the sturdy branches of an apple tree.

"Gone!" he uttered in choked accents. "She is gone!"

For a long moment, the group stared transfixed at the window through which, apparently, Lisette had effected her escape, until an uproar from below broke the spell.

Downstairs, a newcomer was attempting to question the innkeeper regarding his more recent arrivals. As the interrogator posed his questions in English (if one could call it that) and his host spoke only French, this proved to be an exercise in futility. Having failed to communicate any other way, the newcomer, having no French at his command, was now endeavoring to overcome the language barrier through volume.

"Good heavens!" cried Lady Helen, recognizing the voice. *"Ethan!"*

14

If you assure me that your intentions
are honorable.
PIERRE DE BEAUMARCHAIS,
Le Barbier de Séville

Lisette and her flight forgotten, Lady Helen
ran to the top of the stairs and looked down
onto the entryway below. There stood her
husband, gesturing to the innkeeper and
speaking in slow, loud accents, as if ad-
dressing a deaf person.

"A lady — no, no, *la-dy*. A woman," he
explained, sketching a woman's curvaceous
form with his hands. "About this 'igh and
this big around —"

"Ethan!"

He turned toward the sound of her
voice, and Lady Helen was shocked to discover that he looked distinctly green about
the gills.

"Darling, you look dreadful!" she exclaimed. "Are you all right?"

If she had acted distraught, if she had begged him to rescue her, he would have moved heaven and earth to save her. But no, there she stood as if only just risen from her adulterous bed, dress crumpled and hair mussed, fretting over his health as if he had not spend the better part of four hours casting up his accounts into the Channel as he raced to reach her. It was more than flesh and blood could bear.

"Am I all right?" he echoed incredulously, marching somewhat unsteadily up the stairs to confront her. "Me wife runs off with a reprobate, and now she wants to know if I'm *all right?*"

Up came Lady Helen's chin. "I suppose I should be gratified that you tore yourself away from that creature in Green Street long enough to notice I was gone!"

Sir Ethan blinked at her in bewilderment. He had known the Radneys were staunch Tories, but this hatred of Sir Lawrence Latham seemed excessive.

"Why do you stare, Ethan? Did you truly think you could conceal such a connection from your wife? I know it all. I have known ever since I came to London."

Poor Sir Ethan was by this time thoroughly confused, but one thing was becoming increasingly clear: they were *not* discussing politics. "Just what, exactly, are you accusing me of?"

"You have set up that dreadful Hutchins woman as your mistress! You need not bother to deny it. I saw you kissing her in the middle of Green Street."

"Oh, so *that's* it!" Sir Ethan exclaimed as revelation dawned.

"Then you do not deny it!"

"You told me not to bother," he reminded her. "Besides, I wasn't kissing Mrs. 'utchins —"

"You most certainly —"

"She was kissing *me!"*

"You were hardly struggling to free yourself!"

"Not to say this isn't fascinating," Lord Waverly put in, "but may I suggest you find a less public place to continue this discussion? I daresay these gentlemen will not object if you use Lisette's room, as they have business to attend to elsewhere — outside, I think, as none of the rooms here appear to stretch to the requisite twenty paces."

"Twenty paces?" Raoul echoed, turning pale. "But you would not kill the cousin of your wife!"

"No, murder within the family can be so awkward," agreed the earl cordially. "Be assured, I shall shoot you precisely where I intend to."

Seizing Raoul by the collar, Waverly propelled him down the stairs, pausing momentarily when he drew abreast of Sir Ethan.

"Oh, one more thing: when you've finished here — and I quite realize that may take some time — I shall require your services as second, if you've no objection."

Sir Ethan stared at him, flabbergasted. "Let me get this straight. You want *me* to 'elp *you* avenge yourself on the man 'oo kidnapped your wife?" Recalling a similar abduction four years previously in which Lord Waverly had played not nearly so noble a rôle, he hardly knew whether to be offended or amused.

"Believe me, I am fully alive to the irony of the situation. But there is no one else available for the task. Besides, you cannot deny there is a certain poetry about it — a symmetry, if you will."

Taking Sir Ethan's stunned silence for agreement, Lord Waverly gave Raoul a nudge and steered him down the remaining stairs while Étienne brought up the rear.

"You almost 'ave to admire the man's gall," Sir Ethan observed to his wife as he watched the trio depart.

But admiration was not the emotion uppermost in Lady Helen's mind.

"If you have not set Mrs. Hutchins up as a mistress, then *what*, pray, have you been doing in Green Street all this time?"

"Most nights I've been 'aving dinner and talking politics with Sir Lawrence Latham and a few of 'is cronies," Sir Ethan explained, taking her by the arm and leading her into the room so recently vacated by Lord Waverly and the two Frenchmen. Having firmly shut the door behind them, he added, "They want me to stand for election to the 'ouse of Commons — Lord David Markham's seat, to be exact."

"But that's wonderful! And all this time I thought — oh, darling, I've been so miserable!"

"So miserable, in fact, that you were willing to take up with Lord Waverly."

"Only to make you jealous, and in the end, I could not do it, even though I thought you had been unfaithful!"

As she ended this burst of eloquence on a sob, Sir Ethan very wisely put aside his political ambitions and devoted himself instead to the far more urgent task of kissing away his wife's tears.

Upon the completion of this pleasant exercise, Lady Helen gave a sigh of blissful contentment. "And to think of that odious creature accosting you in the street! Surely such behavior is beyond the pale, even in a woman of her profession!"

Sir Ethan, recognizing that the hour of reckoning was now at hand, released his wife with some reluctance. "As to that, love, she didn't exactly *accost* me —"

Lady Helen, seeing guilt writ large upon her husband's expressive countenance, was filled with foreboding. "Ethan! You never accosted *her!*"

"I visited her one time," he said hastily. "Only once, and that not for the reason you think —"

"Indeed?" challenged Lady Helen, filled with righteous indignation. "And what other reason could there be?"

"We talked, that was all. We sat in the parlor and drank tea and — talked."

Lady Helen was not convinced. "About what, pray?"

"You, mostly."

As he enlarged upon this theme, Lady Helen's face grew scarlet with either embarrassment or rage; he knew not which, but had no doubt that he would not be left in ignorance for long.

"Ethan! You discussed all our most intimate — with that — oh, how *could* you?"

" 'ow could I not? Me only other choices were to drive you to an early grave 'aving babies every year, or to take cold baths until me skin rotted off. I didn't care for either one."

Lady Helen's eyes grew round with wonder. "Is *that* why you haven't come near me since Catherine was born?"

"Aye, love, that's it." He drew her into his arms and buried his face in her neck. "I almost lost you once, 'elen. I won't chance it again."

"I was afraid you no longer cared," she whispered, burying her fingers in his hair.

He gave a short laugh. "Oh, I cared, all right! I cared enough to buy a bloomin' fishing boat and chase you clear across the Channel!"

"You bought a boat? For heaven's sake, why?"

"I 'ad to. I'd already missed the packet, and the next one wouldn't sail for hours. So I bought a fishing boat off one of the locals and 'ired 'im to take 'er across." Sir Ethan thought about his maiden voyage, most of which had been spent with his head hanging over the rail. "And a deuced uncomfortable trip I made of it, too."

"Poor darling! No wonder you looked

unwell. But a fishing boat? What on earth are you going to do with it?"

"Burn it!" he said with feeling.

"And so you shall, darling, if that is what you wish. But tell me, did you truly ask Mrs. Hutchins if there was a way to maintain marital relations without having more children?"

"Aye, love, that I did."

"And?" she demanded, agog with eager curiosity. "*Is* there?"

❦

It was a much restored Sir Ethan Brundy who entered the stable yard a short time later to find Lord Waverly and the two Frenchmen awaiting him, along with a dour-looking physician and a mournful priest, presumably there to administer the last rites to the loser. Since only one of the combatants was Catholic, the presence of this individual suggested that Raoul's second had no very great confidence in his ability to best the earl. Sir Ethan had never participated in a duel and was not at all certain that he wished to; however, he had heard them discussed frequently enough at Brooks's to have a fair idea that the first responsibility of a second was to persuade the participants to settle their differences in a less bloodthirsty manner. He was not surprised, therefore, when Étienne came hurrying to meet him.

"Ah, *monsieur!*" cried the Frenchman, wringing his hands in agitation. "Cannot you make milord see reason? We must put a stop to this, you and I!"

"And you think 'e'd listen to me? Not by a long chalk! 'e'd look down that 'aughty nose of 'is and tell me a work'ouse brat couldn't possibly understand an affair of honor. And 'e'd be right, too, come to that."

Étienne found this description so in keeping with his own impressions of Lord Waverly that he made no attempt to refute it. "But think you that he will kill Raoul?"

"I think 'e'll do just what he said 'e would. 'e'll shoot Raoul exactly where 'e intends to."

In fact, Lord Waverly's confrontation with his wife's cousin was almost anticlimactic in its efficiency. Raoul's temperament was much better suited for bullying defenseless young women than for acquitting himself on the field of honor, and his terror at finding himself forced into the latter was such that the result was a foregone conclusion. The paces were stepped off and the signal given, then the two men turned and fired. Lord Waverly's ball passed cleanly through his shoulder (precisely as the earl had intended that it should), and thus Raoul's life, such as it was, was spared.

While the doctor cleaned and bandaged the wound, Waverly restored the pistols to their velvet-lined case, his whole demeanor showing more concern for the well-being of his weapons than for that of his erstwhile adversary. Not until after the doctor and the priest were dismissed from the premises did the earl approach Raoul and his second.

"If you are quite finished," he said, "you may come with me. We are going on a little journey, you and I."

Étienne was moved to protest. "A journey? But Raoul, he is in no condition to travel!"

"Then it is most fortuitous that he will have you along to nurse him back to health. Come, gentlemen, we must waste no more time."

"Where — where are we going?" Raoul rasped feebly, grimacing in pain.

"To the wharf. There is a ship bound for Haiti. When it sets sail, the pair of you will be on it."

"But — but I have not the desire to go to Haiti!" objected Étienne.

Lord Waverly pinned him with a look. "I have assured the repellent Raoul that I would not kill my wife's cousin. I have kept that promise, but I fear — yes, I very much fear that if I should encounter him again, either here or in England, I might, shall we say, forget? And you, I need not remind you, are no blood relation; therefore I need have no such scruples on your account."

Étienne allowed himself to be led to the docks without further protest.

❦

Satisfying though it was to have shipped his wife's tormentors halfway around the world, even this successful maneuver did not change the fact that Lisette was alone and quite possibly lost in a sizable city with which neither of them were very familiar. Although Lord Waverly knew he had married a remarkably resourceful young lady, he also knew that Lisette was far too trusting: one had only to recall how readily she had solicited his escort to England to know that she was no more capable of looking after herself than a babe newborn. The thought of her roaming the streets of Calais alone, an easy mark for thieves, cutthroats, or worse, was enough to make the earl's blood run cold. He would find her, no matter what it took. He would trudge every inch of the city, and beyond it into the surrounding countryside, if he had to. He would not rest until —

I am far too fond of my own comfort to sacrifice it for any female . . .

The memory of his own words brought him up short. He had no illusions that a search such as he proposed would be comfortable; in fact, he had every expectation that it would prove quite the opposite. And yet he was willing — no, *determined* might be a better word — to undertake such a search on Lisette's behalf. The only logical conclusion was that she had somehow become necessary to his comfort. Why? He could think of only one reason: the same one expressed by Lady Helen during the frantic drive to Dover. He had fallen in love with his own wife. How very ironic, that one of the most jaded rakes in the kingdom should succumb to the artless charms of a girl almost half his age! It should have been laughable. And yet the thought of his Lisette at the mercy of the local riff-raff had the effect of wiping the sardonic smile from Waverly's lips. Where was she, and with whom? Was she unharmed?

Morbid imaginings served no useful purpose; what the earl needed was a plan. He would begin with the waterfront inn. Perhaps someone had observed Lisette's escape and noted the direction in which she had set out. Unfortunately, a thorough questioning of the hostel's staff yielded no useful information. The innkeeper recounted Lisette's silent plea for help, and admitted that it was for this reason that he had placed her in a room from which she might escape with relative ease. While he was pleased to know that the young lady had indeed done so, he regretted that he had not seen her again, and so was unable to offer her further assistance.

Other inquiries were equally fruitless. Lisette's flight had apparently coincided with the arrival of the packet from Dover, and amidst the confusion of disembarking passengers, the movements of one mere slip of a girl had gone unremarked. She could not have gone far, he reasoned with perhaps more desperation than logic. She had no money to hire a carriage, even had she had a clear destination in mind. Travelling on foot, she could not have covered much ground. On the other hand, she might have persuaded the driver of a farm cart or some such conveyance to take her up; he could readily imagine her doing just such a thing. If that were the case, she might be anywhere — including her aunt and uncle's home in Amiens.

The mournful peal of church bells seemed to echo Lord Waverly's despair. The bells of Sainte-Jeanne, he supposed, calling the faithful to vespers . . .

The bells of Sainte-Jeanne . . .

No! Surely Lisette would not have sought refuge in a convent, after all she had done to escape one. But Calais was far from Paris, and the sisters of Sainte-Jeanne might never have heard of the goings-on at Sainte-Marie. And where might a young lady find a safer place than at a convent? Somehow this reassuring thought brought no comfort to Lord Waverly. He had a gnawing fear that if Lisette entered a convent a second time, she would not be allowed to escape again.

Well, she would not have to escape; he would go to her and carry her out himself. He would scale the walls, or break them down if he had to, but he would have her back. She was his wife, and no power in heaven or hell would keep him from her.

His mind made up, Waverly set out in the direction from whence had come the sound of the bells. At length he came upon the ancient stone wall surrounding the convent of Sainte-Jeanne. He followed this for some distance until he reached the gate. Finding no one in attendance there, he gave three violent tugs to the bell pull, and when no one appeared in answer to his summons, he rattled the heavy iron gate until the clanging sound echoed off the flagstones of the cloister. A short, plump sister answered the call. Upon spying an elegant (if somewhat rumpled) gentleman seemingly trying to break down the gate, she launched into a flood of impassioned French, of which only one phrase was comprehensible: "But you are a *man!*"

"You are very perceptive," replied Lord Waverly in the same language. "Now have the goodness to surrender my wife."

The stout little nun fairly bristled with indignation. *"C'est impossible, monsieur!* The only women within the walls of Sainte-Jeanne are the brides of Jesus Christ!"

The earl's eyebrows rose in inquiry. "Are you accusing Him of bigamy?"

"Ah! It is blasphemy!"

"Nonsense, Sister Martine." A tall, serene woman entered Waverly's field of vision. "And you, I think, must be Lord Waverly?"

"You know me?" said the earl, taken by surprise.

"Let us say that I have been expecting you — though not, I admit, quite so soon. Come in, *s'il vous plaît.*"

At a signal from her Mother Superior, Sister Martine unlocked the gate, albeit with obvious reluctance. Waverly stepped inside, relieved and yet suspicious at having been granted entrance with such apparent ease.

"And Lisette — ?"

"*Oui, monsieur,* Madame Waverly is here. I believe you will find her in the chapel. Sister Martine will direct you there."

Sister Martine gave him a look which betrayed her willingness to dispatch him to quite a different destination.

"I believe I can find my own way," said the earl. His gaze swept the cloister and alighted on a tall building with stained glass windows in the form of pointed gothic arches. "Surely that must be it?"

"*Oui,* that is it, *monsieur,*" the Mother Superior conceded with a nod. "A fine example of fourteenth-century architecture, *n'est-ce pas?* Be sure to notice the carving over the altar; it is quite remarkable."

Waverly promised to do so, but he was quite uninterested in altars, carved or otherwise. He strode across the cloister, mounted the broad, shallow steps to the chapel, and went inside. The interior was dimly lit, and Waverly stood motionless just inside the door for a moment while his eyes adjusted to the change. The air smelled faintly of incense and burning candles. Sunlight streamed through the stained glass, casting patterns of multicolored light onto the floor. Before the altar knelt a small figure dressed in the white robe and winged headdress of a novice.

"Lisette."

"Milord!" She whirled to face him, eyes alight, but in an instant her transparent joy was replaced by a guarded expression. "Milord," she said again, more restrained this time.

"I've come to take you home, Lisette."

He approached the altar where she knelt and extended a hand to raise her to her feet. She allowed him to lift her up, but made no further move in his direction.

"*Vraiment,* milord, I do not know if I wish to go."

Waverly, taken aback by this declaration, managed to inquire, "May I ask why not?" He had feared the Mother Superior would not permit her to leave; he had never even imagined that Lisette herself might prove unwilling.

"You already have my money; what further need can you have for me?"

Waverly's gentle expression became thunderous. "Who told you such a thing?"

"Étienne told me you married me for my inheritance. Raoul said we were perhaps not truly married at all."

"Raoul lied. Our marriage may have been irregular, but it was — and still is — perfectly legal."

"And Étienne?" she asked, watching him closely. "Did he also lie when he said I was an heiress?"

"It is true that you are an heiress," said the earl, choosing his words with care, "but as God is my witness, I did not know it until well after we were married."

Seeing Lisette struggle with indecision, he possessed himself of her hands. "I will not deny that your fortune was a godsend, Lisette. But it was not the best thing that came from our marriage."

"*Non,* milord?" She was still doubtful, but made no move to withdraw her hands.

"No, Lisette. Since I married you, I have learned to put another person's welfare ahead of my own — at first because I was obliged to do so, but later because I wished it. You rescued me from a life of self-seeking debauchery. One might argue that you saved me from myself."

Lisette snatched her hands out of his clasp and turned away. "And while I save your soul, Lady Hélène will warm your bed, *oui?*"

"Lisette!" exclaimed Lord Waverly, shocked at such forthright speech, and in such a place.

"You think I am too young to know of such things, but I am not."

"It is true that I once desired marriage with Lady Helen. But she was obliged to marry money, and so she wed another. And I —" The earl took her by the shoulders and turned her to face him. "I removed to France, where I spent the next four years drinking myself into a stupor and brooding over my supposed injuries. Only recently have I realized that Lady Helen's chief attraction lay in the fact that I could not have her. Once that obstacle was apparently removed, I discovered the lady had lost much of her appeal."

"You — you no longer love her, milord?" Lisette asked.

"I do not think I ever truly did. That emotion, it seems, was reserved for a very different sort of lady — a very young lady whose innocence, though charming, has caused me more than a few anxious moments. I flattered myself that she needed me. I did not realize just how desperately I needed her until I realized she had been taken from me."

"*Moi?*" she breathed, hardly daring to hope.

"You, Lisette."

Her dark eyes grew round with wonder, and her lips parted in an "O." Lord Waverly, never one to let slip an opportunity, bent and covered her mouth with his own.

"Oh!" cried Lisette in recognition, when at last he released her. "You *did* kiss me that night at the Dorrington ball! I *knew* you did!"

"Yes, I did. And — be warned, *ma petite!* — if you return with me to England, I intend to do a great deal more than that."

As the implications of this threat became clear, Lisette bestowed upon her husband a smile almost blinding in its brilliance, and indicated her approval by flinging herself into his arms.

Epilogue

How much a dunce that has been
sent to roam
Excels a dunce that has been kept
at home!
WILLIAM COWPER,
The Progress of Error

London, 1841

Sir Ethan Brundy, M. P., stood at the edge of the ballroom and surveyed the festivities with a smile of satisfaction, lifting his champagne glass to his wife as she waltzed by in the arms of her brother, the Duke of Reddington. He had, he reflected, a great deal to be thankful for. He was still head over ears in love with the woman he had married in haste a quarter of a century earlier. Both his daughters had made advantageous marriages, and Emily would shortly make him a grandfather. Charles, the eldest of his twin sons, had inherited a modest property from his maternal grandfather, and had turned it into a profitable estate. Thirteen-year-old Benjamin Brundy (alas, even Mrs. Hutchins was not infallible) would be returning to Eton very shortly.

There remained only William, the younger of the twins, to bring a crease to his father's brow. A childhood illness had necessitated Willie's removal from school, so while Charlie set Eton on its ear, his brother was educated more quietly at home. He had eventually outgrown his tendency to sicken, but not without rather unfortunate results. One of these was that he was quite happy to remain buried in Lancashire, where he oversaw the operation of the cotton mill during Sir Ethan's frequent trips to London. Indeed, it had taken no less an event than his parents' twenty-fifth anniversary ball to lure Willie to London, and Sir Ethan suspected that even then his presence was due more to his reluctance to disappoint his mother than to any real desire to sample the delights of Society. As if to put this suspicion to the test, Sir Ethan glanced at the tall young man beside him.

"Would you like a partner, Willie? Miss Williamson is free, and she looks like she's trying to catch your eye. Shall I introduce you?"

From his superior height, Willie Brundy surveyed the partnerless young ladies seated against the opposite wall. The lad had taken his height from his ducal forebears, but in all else — *all* else — he was the image of his father. Spying a predatory-looking redhead simpering at him from behind a lacy fan, he repressed a shudder.

"Good God, no!" he said emphatically. "In fact, I was thinking to make an early night of it. I'm setting out for 'ome at first light."

Even his doting papa could tell that Willie's accent, which never raised an eyebrow in Lancashire, struck a jarring note in a London ballroom. Sir Ethan, hoping to spare his son much of the scorn that he had endured, had once engaged a tutor who assured him of his ability to rid the boy of this social impediment within a month. However, when it was discovered that his methods of instruction relied heavily on the frequent use of a razor strop, Sir Ethan had turned the fellow out on his ear. Willie's accent remained.

"Your mama was 'oping you'd stay on a bit," Sir Ethan told his son. "It wouldn't 'urt you to 'ave a bit of Town bronze, you know."

"Per'aps not, but I don't see that it would 'elp me, either. A waste of time, if you ask me —"

But Sir Ethan did not ask him; in fact, his father was no longer attending him at all, his attention having been claimed by a late arrival.

"I trust you will forgive my tardiness," drawled Lord Waverly. "A late dinner at my club, you know."

"Of course," replied Sir Ethan, accepting the earl's handshake.

"How fortunate for me that the Brundys are such a generous lot! Was it only three weeks ago that your son was presenting mine with — what was it, now? Oh, yes! A black eye, I believe."

Sir Ethan could not but grin at this reference to young Ben's unscheduled holiday from Eton. "Per'aps Viscount Melling will remember in the future not to make unwanted observations on me boy's lineage," he suggested. "Speaking of boys, 'ave you met me second son, Willie?"

Lord Waverly turned his attention to the younger man. "Not since he was in leading strings. I'm sorry to say that he has not improved with age: he still looks far too much like his father."

"I say, Papa — !" exclaimed Willie, taken

aback by this forthright speech.

"Let it go, Willie," advised his father.

"By the bye, have you seen my wife? I promised to meet her here."

"Aye, just a minute ago she was —" Sir Ethan scanned the ballroom once more. "There she is, beside the palm tree."

The set had just ended, and as the violins fell silent, the dancers cleared the floor, giving the earl an unobstructed view of the opposite wall. Beside the palm tree, Lady Waverly sat talking to a dark-haired young lady in a pale pink gown whose bell-shaped skirt emphasized her slender waist. Even at eight-and-thirty, Lisette retained much of the gamine quality that had characterized her at seventeen — a quality also very much in evidence in the young lady who accompanied her.

"Ah, Lord Waverly," said Lady Helen Brundy, retiring from the dance floor to join her spouse. "How lovely to see the two of you cry friends, at least for the occasion."

"Lady Helen," returned the earl, raising her gloved hand to his lips. "Always a pleasure. Tell me, has Lisette utterly given me up?"

"Not at all. William, come make your bow to Lady Waverly. You loved her when you were very small, but you will not remember that."

But Willie Brundy offered no comment. Instead, he stared slack-jawed at the delicate beauty in pink seated beside Lisette. That young lady, as if feeling his eyes upon her, met his gaze across the width of the ballroom and, turning away, began to ply her fan vigorously.

"I say!" said Willie at last. " 'Oo is *that?*"

" 'That,' as you put it, is Lord Waverly's daughter Lady Eugénie."

"That," pronounced Willie with great deliberation, "is the lady I'm going to marry."

Sir Ethan and the earl, staring at one another in mutual horror, made no reply.

About the Author

Sheri Cobb South is the author of five popular young adult novels, as well as a number of short stories in various genres including mystery, young adult, and inspirational. Her first love has always been the Regency, however, and in 1999 she made her Regency debut with the critically acclaimed *The Weaver Takes a Wife*.

Sheri lives near Mobile, Alabama with her husband and two children. You may send her e-mail at Cobbsouth@aol.com, or write to her c/o PrinnyWorldPress, P.O. Box 248, Saraland, AL 36571.